M000317745

CONTENTS

CORGI CASE FILES

CASE OF THE

ABANDONED BONES
BOOK 10

J.M. POOLE

Secret Staircase Books

Case of the Abandoned Bones

Corgi Case Files, Book 10

By

J.M. Poole
www.AuthorJMPoole.com

A busy corgi has a happy owner!

Case of the Abandoned Bones
Published by Secret Staircase Books, an imprint of
Columbine Publishing Group, LLC
PO Box 416, Angel Fire, NM 87710

Book layout and design by Secret Staircase Books
Cover images by Felipe de Barros, Yevgen Kachurin

* * *

Publisher's Cataloging-in-Publication Data

Poole, J.M.
Case of the Abandoned Bones / by J.M. Poole.
p. cm.
ISBN 978-1649140371 (paperback)
ISBN 978-1649140388 (e-book)

1. Zachary Anderson (Fictitious character)--Fiction. 2.
Pomme Valley, Oregon—Fiction. 3. Cozy mystery—Fiction. 4.
Corgi dogs—Fiction. 5. Amateur sleuth—Fiction. I. Title

Corgi Case Files mystery series : Book 10.
Poole, J.M., Corgi Case Files mysteries.

BISAC : FICTION / Mystery & Detective.

813/.54

ACKNOWLEDGMENTS

Kudos must be given to my close circle of family, friends, and readers who have volunteered their time to help me get the book polished as much as possible. Jason, Carol, Mefe, Caryl, Diane, Elizabeth, and Louise. Thank you very much for all your help!

Another shoutout to my niece, Kaylee, who helped me flesh out the character of Lucky Dawg, and was later changed to Red Dawg. Believe it or not, Red Dawg was actually based on a real-life person, only known as "Set 'Em Up" and as of this writing, Set 'Em Up's mine is still missing.

I hope you enjoy the story! Happy reading!

For Giliane -
Thoughtful quotation to be inserted here!

What can I say that I haven't said
already? Love you, babe!

ONE

W hat's the latest? You asked me out here for a reason, so I can only assume construction must have hit some type of a snag. Level with me. What'd they find? Did something break? They expect me to pay for it, don't they? Huh? Huh? Well, you can tell them ..."

"Whoa, Zack," my companion told me, chuckling. "Take it down a notch. There aren't any snags. Nothing has broken. In fact, everything is right on schedule."

"Oh. Really?"

"I heard about what you went through last week."

"Yeah, that was something. Wait. Which incident are you referring to?"

"There's more than one?" the second voice incredulously asked.

I nodded. "Yep. Three. Which one are you talking about?"

"I was referring to being forced out of a plane,"

the second voice clarified. "At gunpoint. Dare I ask what the other two were about?"

"Oh. Well, there was white water rafting down the Rascal."

My winemaster shrugged. "That's really not too bad. Provided you avoid David's Drop, that is."

"And there was bungee jumping off some bridge in Central Oregon," I added.

"You went bungee jumping? You're kidding. Which bridge?"

I shrugged. "I forget the name of it. I think it was called Peter something."

My companion grabbed me by the arm and pulled me to a stop.

"The Peter Skene Ogden bridge?"

"Hey, that's the one. I won't ever forget that. Someone almost died out there."

"But … I just read about that in the newspaper not that long ago! You were there? How's the guy doing?"

"C2? He'll pull through, only his road to recovery is going to be a long one."

"He wouldn't be the guy you were telling me about yesterday, would he? The guy you hired to handle all of the winery's social media accounts?"

"Yep, that's him."

"Do we really need to have that much of a presence online?"

"It couldn't hurt, right? Caleb's job will be to monitor Lentari Cellars' accounts, answer questions, and keep updated content on our pages."

Caden stared at me for a few moments before his face broke out in a smile.

"You're doing this to help him out. Let me guess. He can't afford to take time off from work?"

"Guilty as charged. I found out, from the former leader of the Daredevils, he had been let go from his job just a few days ago. He hasn't found anything since. So, he's our new IT guy."

"IT guy, too, huh? Well, good. That means I don't have to be the one you keep calling when you can't get your printer to work."

"Oh, puh-lease. I don't call you that often, do I?"

In response, Caden pulled out his cell phone from his pocket and showed me his call history. Of the dozen or so incoming calls on his screen, my name was there at least seven or eight times. Cringing, I offered my companion a smile.

"Yeah, well … okay. Sorry 'bout that. What can I say? That flippin' printer has a mind of its own, and it has decided it hates me."

"I still can't believe you went bungee jumping. What was it like?"

"A once-in-a-lifetime experience," I confirmed. "And one that I don't ever plan on experiencing again. Unless, of course, I get a gun shoved in my face."

"Did someone really force you to jump out of a plane?" Caden asked. We crested the top of the north hill and stopped. "I'm not sure how I would have handled that."

3

"The same way I handled it, I'm sure."

"And how did you handle it?" Caden curiously asked.

"By peeing my pants and screaming like a little girl all the way down."

Caden laughed out loud.

"In all honesty, it really wasn't as bad as people made it out to be," I said.

"He didn't have a gun?"

"Oh, he had a gun, all right."

"I see. It wasn't loaded?"

"I'm pretty sure it was loaded," I confirmed.

"But, he wasn't going to use it?"

I shrugged. "I'm pretty sure he was going to use it, too."

"Then I disagree," my companion said. "It was just as bad as I've heard. In fact, I think it's worse. I can't even begin to fathom why you'd want to do something like that."

"I was helping out a friend," I told my wine-master. "He was having a mid-life crisis. Wanted to prove he was still young at heart, I guess. Don't get old, pal. It sucks."

First things first. Introductions. My name is Zack Anderson. I'm the owner of Lentari Cellars, the private winery Caden Burne and I were currently touring. Actually, if you want to get technical, the two of us were leisurely cruising past the new warehouse that was slowly being constructed. For some reason, I thought we'd be further along than having less than a quarter of the framing in place. But, based on how many inspections have to be performed, in the correct order, I really shouldn't complain. Caden was doing a remarkable job of keeping the contractors in line and making certain the winery ran as smoothly and efficiently as possible.

I honestly don't know what I'd do without the guy.

"Where are you taking me?" I politely inquired, as we left the main winery building behind and headed north.

Row after row of healthy vines stretched out in all directions. Big fat clusters of grapes could be seen on each and every single plant. This was truly going to be our largest harvest yet.

Caden took a hand off the wheel of the John Deere Gator he was currently driving and pointed. I glanced in the direction we were headed and nodded. For some reason, my winemaster wanted to show me the new orchard he had planted. Wanting to expand the winery's offerings, Caden had talked me into investing a sizeable amount of money on bringing in large, older fruit trees of all sorts: apples, peaches, pears, and so on. Planted next to our new fruit trees was nearly a full acre of various berry bushes, from marionberry to gooseberry. Looking forward to snacking on some fresh fruit, hot off the tree and/or bush, I couldn't sign the checks fast enough.

"They're coming along nicely," I observed, as we slowed to inspect a row of apple trees.

"They're doing better than I could have hoped," Caden agreed. "There. Do you see this? This here, along the left of the road?"

"Looks like bushes," I observed. I turned and pointed at the matching rows behind it. "In fact, they look just like those, and those, and those over there."

"Can you identify them?" Caden challenged.

I shrugged and turned back to the closest row of berry bushes. After silently studying them for a few minutes, I turned to my companion and nodded.

"Marionberry."

"Nope. Those are over there."

"Gooseberry?"

"Nope."

"Umm, salal berries?"

For those who may not know, salal berries are a lesser known, native-to-Oregon berry which taste like sweet blueberries with a hint of grape thrown in. And, I can actually say that I've tried a piece of salal berry pie. That was back when we actually had a bakery-related murder. I don't know about you, but death by muffin doesn't really sound like a bad way to go, does it?

"They're on the list for next year," Caden confirmed. "Now isn't the time of year to be planting anything. And, for the record, I'm surprised you've heard of them. I mean, let's face it. They're not a popular berry."

"I know they're not commonly known, but

that doesn't mean I haven't heard of them. And, I'm sorry to say, not in a good way."

Caden turned to me and cringed. "I have a feeling I don't want to know."

"Well, um, it had to do with..."

"Were Sherlock and Watson involved?" Caden hastily interrupted.

"They were," I confirmed.

"Then it's 'nuff said for me."

Sherlock and Watson. Where do I start with those two? Well, for those who are not familiar with my two dogs, let me give you a brief history. They're both corgis. Pembroke Welsh Corgis, to be exact. They're the breed of corgis who typically don't have any tails. Their ears are rounded, their legs are short, and they have personalities as large as Saint Bernards.

I adopted my two corgis shortly after moving to Pomme Valley from Phoenix, Arizona. And by *shortly*, I mean in less than twenty-four hours of setting foot in this small town. I adopted my little boy, Sherlock, after being suckered into it by none other than Harrison Watt, my best friend from high school. How the two of us managed to find ourselves in the same small town, hundreds of miles away from Arizona, still mystifies me. Well, Harry had become a veterinarian, and seeing how he was responsible for finding 'furever homes' for rescue dogs, he had guilted me into taking Sherlock.

Now, several years later, I can't imagine my life

without my dogs. Oh, I suppose you're wondering about Watson. Well, she came to me not long after … yes, you heard correctly. Watson is a she. My little girl has gone by other names, but after coming to live with us, I had given her the name Watson. Why? Well, it went with Sherlock, of course.

Now, for the amazing part.

Those two little dogs have an incredible skill. They solve mysteries, be it murder or robbery, or anything else you can think of. In fact, they've become so adept at solving cases that the local police department have made us official police consultants.

Somehow, and I have never figured out how, those two dogs can zero in on clues so trivial that, for all intents and purposes, it looks like nonsense to an outsider. However, once the details of the case are laid out, the 'corgi clues' as I'm now starting to call them, inevitably pan out. Every. Single. Time.

I'm stumped. My good friend Vance Samuelson, a detective on the Pomme Valley police force, is also stumped. Sherlock and Watson have solved murder cases, located stolen loot, and have even located people who don't want to be found.

How?

I honestly have no idea. The only rule we have, when working a case, is to be on the lookout for the omniscient *woof*. Yep, that may sound laughable at best, but when you're driving around town, looking for stolen property, or trying to find a missing fugitive, hearing one (or both) of the dogs woofing at something will always warrant a second look. Oftentimes, I'm driving and I don't have the ability to bring my Jeep to a safe stop. So, what do I do? The next best thing: take pictures.

There have been many occasions when those pictures can (and will) break a case wide open. Therefore, I pay attention to whatever catches my dogs' attention, regardless of how silly or insignificant it may be. Take the last case the dogs and I worked. Photos of trash from a campsite, the backside of a guy in camouflage pants, and a number of other shots all looked as though they would never be related to an ongoing murder case. Yet, they all were, and somehow the dogs knew.

Still fresh in my mind, since that particular case had just wrapped up a few days ago, the stunts I ended up doing with a group of young thrill-seekers still continued to amaze me. As I mentioned before, those stunts were white-water rafting, bungee jumping, and sky diving. Put those three activities together and I guaran-damn-tee you the first thing you're going to think of is mid-life crisis. Well, believe it or not, I wasn't going through one but my aforementioned detective friend, Vance, was. He talked me and Harry into joining the Dysfunctional Daredevils in an effort to locate an escaped mass murderer. Undercover, of course.

Jillian, my fiancée, was none too pleased with me, but did support my decision to help out my friends. Now, with those events safely behind me, but in the not-too-distant past, I was eager for some down time, only as you will shortly see, it wasn't in the books. Life, I'm sorry to say, has a plethora of ways to deliver reality checks. For me, they were the equivalent of a swift kick to the family jewels.

The all-terrain vehicle came to a sudden stop. Lost in my own thoughts, I had to blink a few times to clear my head. Slowly turning to see where we were, I nodded. We were out in the northern fields, which had been included in the winery's expansion a year or so back. This particular field once belonged to a former neighbor of mine. Tim Parson formerly farmed this land but had since retired and moved away. His family, desiring nothing to do with farming, sold the farmland off to several people, one of them obviously being me. Thanks to Tim's oldest son's generosity, Lentari Cellars had increased from fifteen acres to an astounding fifty, seemingly overnight.

For close to a year, the northern field sat vacant. Now, as the two of us sat in the Gator, looking over the empty field, I could only imagine what Caden had in store. More fruit trees? Berry bushes? Perhaps something completely different?

"What're your thoughts?" I wanted to know. "Plan on putting more fruit trees out here?"

"Honestly? I haven't gotten that far yet."

"You haven't? I'm surprised, amigo. Well, why are we out here?"

Caden turned and pointed at a mound of large, nearby boulders. "Oh, I have a few things in mind for this land. However, that is nowhere on my list."

"Hmm? Are you talking about those big rocks?"

Caden nodded. "Exactly. Whether we continue to plant more fruit trees, or use the land to plant more vines, those rocks have gotta go."

"And you're telling me this because I need to put rock removal on my To Do list?"

Caden shrugged before he looked my way. "Aren't you the one who loves working in the new tractor?"

"I do," I confirmed. I then pointed at the closest rock, which looked to be the size of my Jeep. "I think even those may be a little on the large side. There's no way the tractor could pick that thing up."

"You could if you break them apart," Caden said.

"And how would you suggest I do that? Smack it with the loading bucket?"

Caden chuckled. "No. I was thinking you could rent an attachment for it. They do have specialty tools a tractor can use, you know."

Intrigued, I nodded. "I really hadn't thought of that. All right. Maybe there's something I can use on the tractor which could break apart those rocks. I'll see what I can do."

The following day, I was at the controls of my John Deere 5083EN tractor. Sitting comfortably inside the cab, I glanced over at the buddy seat and gave each of the corgis a pat on the head. Then, I turned my attention to what had replaced the bucket. A hydraulic hammer, which to me looked like a squat black box with a long, thick spike angled down, was poised directly over the first of the large rocks I had intended to break apart. One of the winery's interns, Douglas, wanted to accompany me with the flatbed truck, only I pointed out that I was breaking apart the rocks at this stage, not lifting them. That would come tomorrow.

Now, inches away from seeing what this baby could do, I glanced again at the dogs and prayed the cab of this tractor would keep the majority of the noise outside. After all, I didn't want to spook either of the dogs, and if it proved too loud, then I'd have to take them back to the house. Verifying the hydraulic pressure was where it should be, I eased the tip of the spike down and engaged the hammer.

First and foremost, I should point out the dogs had absolutely no problem with the noise. It was loud, yes, but then again, it could have been so much worse. What I found disconcerting was the simple fact that it felt like a giant had come up behind me, grabbed a hold of the tractor, and had just shaken the snot out of it. Everything in the cab which wasn't bolted down was flung up into the air, before falling noisily back to the ground.

I grinned at Sherlock and Watson, who had just given themselves a solid shake to dislodge the dust and debris which had settled on their coats.

"That was something, wasn't it? Wow. I think that just rattled my teeth loose. Okey dokey, let's see what we got. Think there's any chance we broke it in half on the first try?"

I was ignored. Apparently, with this spiked-gizmo moving this way and that outside, the dogs thought there was some type of monster attached to the tractor, and assumed it needed to be watched. Shrugging, I leaned forward in my seat to inspect the damage.

A tiny divot, no bigger than a golf ball, was visible on the huge rock's surface. Surprised and elated that I'd get to use this mechanical spike for much longer than anticipated, I resumed hammering away at the boulder. With the size of the dust cloud this thing was kicking up, I was surprised there was any dirt left on the ground.

"We're gonna have to give this thing a bath when all this is over," I told the dogs nearly thirty minutes later.

Patience won out. A deep, jagged crack was visible, which effectively split the boulder in half. Additionally, it only took another ten minutes of hammering before one of the halves split again, reducing each section to about the size of a small loveseat. Figuring that was about the limit of what my tractor could lift, I made short work of the other half of the boulder.

Intent on dragging the pieces out of the way, thus giving me access to the next set of large boulders, I grabbed my gloves and a set of chains. It took nearly twenty minutes to attach the chains and drag the four broken pieces of rock away from the rest. Rubbing my hands together, I returned to the cab.

"That wasn't so bad, was it?" I asked the dogs. Positioning the tractor by the next large boulder, I maneuvered the hydraulic hammer into place. "If we can get these two broken down, and then maybe those three over there, I'd say that'd be a good day's work."

Once again, I was ignored. The dogs only had eyes for what was happening on the other side of the glass. Looking back on the events of the day, I definitely should have paid more attention to what the corgis were doing.

As the afternoon passed, with me busy at the controls of the tractor, my mind started to drift. After all, it didn't really require too many brain cells to pull this lever here and rotate that knob there, while pushing a few pedals down there. So, I started reflecting on how much life had changed for me, and if you had known me several years ago, you'd say the difference was as significant as night and day.

Several years ago, I had been living in my home state of Arizona, in the great city of Phoenix. I had recently lost my wife of over twenty years to a horrific automobile accident. I had been a best-selling author, but my sales had begun to drop. Why? My depressive attitude transferred to my books. I had been told they weren't as good, and I had to admit, they weren't.

I was in a deep, depressing funk, and thankfully, I could see that. That was when one phone call changed my life forever: I had inherited a winery.

Fast forward to the present day. Here I was, sitting in a tractor, of all things, in an attempt to clear the land so my winemaster could figure out what he wanted to do with it. My winery. It may be mine on paper, but I fervently believed there were two owners, and no, I wasn't thinking of my late wife, but my very-current fiancée, Jillian.

I was engaged to be married. My books were selling like hotcakes once more, and I had recently hit the *USA Today* bestseller's list, a feat I hadn't accomplished in several years. I owned two dogs who at present were sitting beside me in the cab of my tractor.

Sherlock and Watson. My life had already started improving for the better when those two corgis came trotting into the picture. Both were rescues, only I steadfastly believe they rescued me, not the other way around. They lived with me, kept me company, and were fantastic listeners.

Most of the time.

The cab of the tractor gave a mighty shake. Watson slid off her chair and would have taken a hard fall but, thankfully, I managed to catch her before that could happen. Gently placing her back on the seat, I gave the affectionate girl a pat on the head, and then did the same for Sherlock when he glanced our way.

"Better watch yourselves. This last boulder is huge. Flat, but huge. I thought we had finally broken through, but the hammer slipped. Sorry about that, guys. I'll pay better attention next time."

As if either dog didn't believe me, both sat up on the seat and stared — intently — at the massive slab of stone below.

"Ready for round two? All right. Here we go."

A second tremor shook the cab, but it wasn't as strong as the previous one. This time, I was rewarded with a large crack on the slab's surface. A few more strikes by the hammer's spike and I saw the point sink into the rock, suggesting the slab might not be as thick as I had originally thought. Pulling the hammer up and out of the stone, I let the tractor idle and hopped out to take a look.

Both corgis had their noses pressed to the glass as they watched.

"Hmm. Doesn't look like much, guys. I may have thought this was the biggest sarcophagus in the world, but I think it's just my overactive imagination. Back in your seat, you two. Let's break it into a few more pieces."

Once the slab had been broken into five pieces, and I had just dragged the second chunk out of the way, both dogs perked up again. In fact, Sherlock started howling.

Ever hear a corgi howl? It's a funny sight to behold. It was all I could do not to laugh at the poor guy. Watson, for her part, seemed to be wriggling with anticipation, almost as if Vance was here with his bag of doggie biscuits.

"What's going on with you two? There's nothing to see, okay? I ... Sherlock? Stop pawing the windows. You're gonna get it dirty. Well, dirtier than it already is."

Sherlock threw back his head and howled again, only it wasn't high-pitched. Quite the opposite. The howl was low, long, and full of syllables.

"Awwooooo...woo....wooooooo!"

Bemused, I turned to my tri-colored corgi and gave him a friendly scratch. I checked the time and decided we all needed a break. After all, the corgis had been in the cab with me for over three hours. Perhaps they needed a potty break?

Reaching in, I twisted the key and shut the engine down. "Fine, is that better? Here. Would you two like to go running around? I think I might have a ball in here somewhere, so maybe we could..."

I trailed off as both corgis took off like a bat out of hell. Both circled around the tractor and zeroed in on the patch of pale earth that had been exposed with the partial removal of the slab. Watson yipped her encouragement as Sherlock went full-on prairie dog on me. He shoved his snout down low, hunched his back, and dug like he believed I had been trapped by an avalanche. Dirt, scraps of weeds, and bits of rock were thrust between the corgi's squat rear legs as the hole Sherlock was digging widened to four feet. Five minutes later, he was still at it.

For the record, I had considered putting a stop to the digging at least five times, only something prevented me from doing so. I think it had something to do with the urgency with which Sherlock was digging. What would possess him to dig frantically in that spot for so long?

"I can only assume you've found something," I mused, as I leaned against the tractor's front wheel and watched the proceedings.

Sherlock finally paused in his digging. He looked up at me, gave himself a thorough shake, and then glanced over at Watson. He yipped once and promptly resumed digging. This time, however, Watson joined him, only she was digging in a completely different place.

I was about to laugh and take a photo for posterity's sake when a thought occurred. What if Sherlock had found something? What if that slab had been some type of burial stone, and there was some type of tomb below it? Might some type of ancient people have once lived on this land and used it to bury their dead?

Eww.

What had Caden always told me about wine? That it absorbs the nutrients and flavors of all that's around it? The existence of ancient burial grounds would definitely raise a question or two from my buyers, that's for sure.

"Sherlock? I'm having second thoughts, dude. Maybe you shouldn't dig so close to the other pieces of that slab. Come on, let's get back inside the cab, okay? Oh, man. You're absolutely covered with dirt. What's Jillian going to say? She's coming over tonight for a nice, romantic dinner. What's she going to say when she sees you two?"

Neither dog bothered looking up.

I snapped my fingers a few times in the hopes that it'd get the dogs' attention. But, to have both of them pause at the same time and look up at me, with the same annoyed expression on their face? Jillian would have ended up laughing her rear off. Me? I shook my head and hooked a thumb at the tractor.

"All right, that's enough. We need to think about heading back. I want both of you to…"

I trailed off as I noticed what was in Sherlock's hole. It was off-white, domed, and the size of a mini-basketball. Sherlock, satisfied that I had now given the situation my full attention, shook himself off a second time and stepped back. Watson joined him a few moments later and, together, they watched me kneel down on the ground and scrape away the dirt with my gloved hands.

"This had better not be what I think it is," I grumbled to myself as I picked up a nearby rock and used it to chip away the hard earth surrounding the object.

Several large pieces of dirt broke away. Once I

had removed them, the majority of the object was revealed, causing me to curse violently as I jerked to my feet. I stared at the object before picking up both dogs and placing them in the tractor's cab. Turning to look back into the hole, I groaned and pulled out my cell. While I placed the call to my detective friend, Vance Samuelson, Sherlock and Watson crowded the window and stared intently at me. I'd like to say that this was the first time the dogs have discovered something like this on my property, but anyone familiar with my history in PV will know that's a lie. This was just peachy.

The empty eye sockets of a bone-white skull leered evilly up at me.

TWO

Y ou're up, Watson. It's your turn to ... Sherlock? Let her have the ball, okay? Thank you. Now, why don't you ... Sherlock? I said drop it, pal. Poor Watson hasn't had a chance to play with the ball yet. Be a good boy and let her have it."

I swear that dog held the ball in his mouth as long as necessary to ensure it was completely coated with saliva. Dropping the soggy tennis ball at my feet, he looked defiantly up at me as if to say, you wanted it, there it is. Let's see you touch that nasty mess, dad.

Two days had passed. We were currently at one of PV's two parks, trying to burn off some excess energy (and help me get my mind off of things). All you dog owners will back me up when I say, if you don't give your dogs something to do, then they'll find ways to entertain themselves. Trust me, you really don't want that. Seeing how the last couple of days have been pretty hectic, and I haven't been able to spend too much time with either of the corgis, an excursion outside for some playtime was warranted.

My thoughts kept drifting back to the talk of the town, namely the discovery of human remains on my land. Who was the unlucky person? How did the bones end up under that huge rock? Did I have any insight as to how long they'd been there?

Thankfully, the dogs were there and kept pulling me back to reality. Typically, Sherlock wasn't this ornery whenever we played with a ball. Now, for some reason, it was like he was deliberately pushing my buttons. He wouldn't share with Watson. He wouldn't give me the ball. When he did drop it at my feet, he'd dart in to grab the ball before I could. I knew I couldn't get mad at him, seeing how I knew what he was doing. The clever little dog was trying to distract me. I think he could tell every time my mind wandered, and he felt it necessary to steer it back on track.

After ten minutes or so of idly tossing the ball around, both corgis perked up and turned, in unison, to look at the street. Noticing that something had caught their attention, I automatically looked that way. However, I couldn't tell what either of them were looking at. Confused, I looked back at my dogs and waggled the ball.

"Guys? Over here. What are you looking at? There's nothing over there except passing cars. Did one of your many admirers drive by?"

Sherlock whipped his head around at me, whined, and then returned his attention to the street.

"But, we're not working a case!" I protested.

Watson nudged my leg. By the time I looked down at my red and white corgi, Watson had already resumed staring at the street, too.

I groaned. "Fine. You win. Here. Want me to take some pictures? Would either of your Royal Majesties care to indicate what I should be looking for?"

Both dogs ignored me.

"Fine. I see how I rate."

I slowly panned the street with my cell phone, taking a series of pictures as I did so. I really hadn't a clue what I was looking for, so I made sure to hit all areas of the street. Once done, I was finally able to tuck my phone away.

Unsurprisingly, this seemed to mollify the dogs.

"I'll never understand you two."

Right about then, a group of middle-schoolers wandered by. There were four girls and one boy. One of the girls, whom I guessed was the ringleader since the rest of the group came to an immediate stop once she did, approached me and asked permission to pet the dogs. Surprised by the girl's good manners, I nodded.

"Is this a boy or a girl?" the girl wanted to know.

"Boy," I answered.

"Aren't you a cute boy?" the girl cooed, which

caused Sherlock to roll over onto his back and wait for a belly rub. Not to be outdone, Watson thrust her nose under the girl's arm and nudged it up and out of the way. Moments later, my timid little girl wedged herself in between Sherlock and the girl, forcing the twelve-year-old to pet her, and not him.

"That one is a female," I pointed out.

"What are their names, mister?" one of the other girls asked.

I pointed at Sherlock. "That one, the male, with the black, orange, and white coat is Sherlock. He's the one who hasn't blinked since you picked up the ball. Under your arm there is Watson."

"Omigod!" the girl cried, as she looked adoringly at the two dogs. "Sherlock and Watson! I should have known! Lisa, did you hear that? Do you know who these two are?"

The rest of the gang crowded close and began heaping praise and adoration upon the two corgis.

"These dogs are famous!" another girl exclaimed, as she whipped out her cell phone and started taking pictures. "I am so posting this online. Jenna, squat down next to them. Put an arm around each of them. Perfect! I'll bet these pics will go viral by the end of the day!"

Viral? Whatever happened to just sharing the picture with your friends? Whatever.

An excited squeal from one of the girls had me looking back at the group of kids. They were all kneeling on the soft grass and petting both of the dogs. I noticed the soggy tennis ball next to Sherlock and pointed at it.

"Both Sherlock and Watson love chasing after that ball. Care to do the honors?"

"Can we?" the girl excitedly asked. "You don't mind?"

"Do you see how soggy that ball is?" I countered. "Trust me, you'd be doing me a favor."

"Thank you, Mr. Anderson," the girl gushed, admitting to me she knew who I was.

She grabbed the tennis ball and hurriedly rose to her feet. Both corgis were on their feet in a flash. Sherlock sensed there had been a shakeup with his playmates and, without looking back at me, chased after the girl and her friends. Watson, bless her heart, waited by my side. She looked up at me, yipped once, and wriggled with anticipation.

"Go on, girl. Go have fun. And ... you just earned yourself a treat when we get home."

Watson tore off after Sherlock and the kids. In the meantime, I headed for the closest park bench which would allow me to keep an eye on the dogs. Leaning back, I shaded my eyes and watched the dogs frolic with the youngsters. Should I be worried something would happen to them?

The answer was simple: no.

Everyone in this town seemed to know the dogs and all of them, I might add, wanted to be their friends. As for me, I was perfectly comfortable to remain on the sidelines and remain unknown. Let someone else get all the attention.

Now, that typically worked for me except for days like this. My name, and my winery, were all anyone could talk about. Just because a few bones were located on my property, everybody wanted to freak out.

Well, okay. Sure, they might've found over two hundred bones, but that's beside the point, isn't it? Yes, that might mean they found a complete skeleton, but was that any reason to dig up nearly half an acre? And cordon off nearly five acres of surrounding land?

On the plus side, the city of Pomme Valley very kindly removed the last of the large boulders from that section of the property. It was Chief Nelson, himself, who suggested they remove the rest of the boulders, just to see if there were any other remains hidden in the ground. Fortunately, there weren't. I still had the feeling I was gonna get the bill from the crew who had been brought in to break up the stones.

Oh, well. It beats me having to do it.

My cell phone rang, which caused me to jump. Glancing at the display, I saw that Vance was on the other end, not Jillian as I had hoped. Steeling myself for some bad news, I took the call.

"Hey, Vance. What's up?"

"Hey, Zack. How're you doing?"

"I'll be doing a lot better once I hear you tell me that you won't be arresting me again."

"For finding some old bones on your property? Property that has only been yours for barely two years? Relax, buddy. You're not being charged."

"Music to my ears. All right, what's up? What can I do for you?"

"It's more about what I can do for you. Brace yourself. We're pretty sure we know who was found buried on your land."

"Oh? And you're only *pretty sure*?"

"Before I tell you, I think I should warn you that, if I'm right, then this will likely generate even more publicity than all of your other cases, combined."

"No kidding? Okay, I'll bite. Who do you think it is? Jimmy Hoffa?"

Vance laughed. "Hardly. Rumor has it those bones belong to Charles Hanson."

"Who?"

"Charles Hanson. Seriously? You don't know who he is?"

"Never heard of him," I confessed.

"Oh. That's right. You haven't lived in PV long enough to know who he is. I keep forgetting. Charles Hanson has to be PV's most infamous missing person's case. Even though it had never been proven foul play was involved, I think everyone knows he met his untimely end. Remember me telling you the last murder in PV was over fifty years ago? Well, I was referring to this case."

My eyebrows shot up. "I always thought you were making that part up."

"Nope. This case happened over fifty years ago. BZ."

"BZ?" I repeated, confused.

"Before Zack."

"Kiss my butt, pal. Bad luck just follows me around, okay?"

"Sure. If you say so. Anyway, once we get a confirmation of the identity, and the press learns who you found on your property, then they're gonna freak out."

"Well, as long as they know I had nothing to do with it, then I shouldn't have anything to worry about, right?" My friend fell silent. "Vance? Still with me?"

"I'm here. What you have to understand, pal, is that the press are notorious for latching on to a story and sticking with it."

"What does that mean? Do you know something I don't?"

"I recommend screening your calls for the next couple of days."

"What? Why?"

"Gotta go. We'll talk later."

An hour later, official word of the remains' identification must have officially gone out, because the phone calls began. My cell phone started ringing, and no matter how many times I sent the call to voice mail, it wouldn't stop. Plus, it wasn't even the same number. Each time I looked at the display, a different number met my eyes. I'd like to say that my phone has never rung this much in my life, only that wouldn't be true. After the first time a body had been discovered in my winery, my phone had rung for several days straight. Following the discovery of the bones out in the northern fields, my phone didn't stop ringing for two days straight.

Vance clearly knew this was going to happen. The crazy thing was, not only were calls coming from various news outlet in PV, but from outside PV as well. Reporters from Medford, Bend, and even as far away as Portland, wanted my take on the ramifications of my discovery.

I quickly grew tired of answering the same questions, over and over. No, I can't confirm Mr. Hanson had been buried on my land. No, I didn't think the guy I bought that land from knew he was out there, either. No, I won't be closing the winery.

On and on it went.

An hour later, all three of us were exhausted. They, having run around the park like lunatics for almost two hours straight, had accomplished what we set out to do, which was to namely tucker them out. As for me, mine was more of a mental exhaustion. We had just made it back to the house when I finally decided to turn my cell back on. For all I knew, Jillian might have been trying to get ahold of me. But, the instant I did, the darn thing started ringing again. By now, I must've sent nearly fifty calls to voice mail before getting fed up with the thing and shutting it off. None of the calls had recognizable area codes, and as a result, I wasn't planning on answering any of them. Hoping against hope this particular call was familiar, I checked the display.

Well, the area code said it was from this area, only I didn't recognize the prefix. It had to be a local number, only I didn't know who. Had the news spread that quickly? Could it be someone who might know something? Against better judgement, I took the call.

"Hello?"

"Is this Mr. Zachary Anderson, owner of Lentari Cellars?"

"Yep. Who's this?"

"My name is Kara Averson, from the *Arizona Republic*. Would you mind if I ask you a few questions?"

"Well, Ms. Averson, as you can imagine, I've been dealing with quite a few calls lately. I really don't have any desire to answer any more questions."

I heard a dejected sigh on the phone.

"But," I continued, "you asked politely, and I respect that. So, I'll answer a few."

"Thank you, Mr. Anderson. Okay, first question. Are you familiar with the case of Mr. Charles Hanson?"

"Not until about two hours ago," I confirmed.

My answer must have caught the reporter off guard.

"I-I'm sorry?"

"You heard me right. A friend of mine from the PVPD called to let me know the suspected identity of the person found on my property was some guy by the name of Charles Hanson. I guess I haven't lived in PV long enough to know his history. And, for the record, you guys are quick. If you don't mind me asking a question, how could you possibly have learned so fast? Your newspaper is headquartered in Phoenix. I know. I used to live there. Nothing has been confirmed, which means you're calling about a rumor. How did you find out so fast?"

The reporter laughed, which helped to put me at ease.

"Everything is computerized now," Kara informed me. "I pay top dollar to be notified about certain stories incorporating very specific keywords. In your case, anyone with an Arizona connection, linked to a murder case, will eventually end up in my Inbox. As a reporter, speed is an issue. If I don't act fast, then someone else can scoop the story and I'm out of luck. And, if I am allowed to also say 'for the record' I've seen your name in my inbox quite a bit."

It was my turn to laugh. "Did my friend put you up to this? He thinks I'm a jinx."

To best describe what happened next, I need to interrupt here for just a moment to introduce a couple of new electronic devices which now call the winery home. First and foremost, I have several wireless security cameras stationed around the house. No one can sneak up on my property without their picture being taken and uploaded to a safe, secure account online. Next, for my last birthday, I was given a device which could interface to the Internet and a number of my electronic gizmos around the house. That included, of course, my camera system. Whenever someone tripped a camera, the snapshot would not only be uploaded, but also displayed on the device. Finally, my new toy could take control of the camera and open up a two-way intercom system, thus allowing me to talk to anyone who happens to be standing in front of said camera.

The reason why I told you all of that is simple. While I was on the phone with what had to be the politest, nicest reporter I have ever talked to in my life, my electronic toy on my desk chirped. Someone had stepped in front of one of my cameras. Glancing over, I saw the smiling face of my lovely fiancée as she ascended the front steps of my house and disappeared through the front door.

"Ms. Averson? Pardon me a moment. I need to place you on hold. Is that okay?"

"Take all the time you need, Mr. Anderson."

"Thanks." I muted the call and then headed toward the living room just as Jillian was setting something down on the coffee table. I blinked a few times as I stared at the object. It looked like a cloth-covered basket. "Hi, Jillian. You're a sight for sore eyes."

Jillian went sympathetic. "Rough day?"

I shrugged. "It's looking up. What do you have there?"

Jillian whipped the towel off the object, confirming my suspicions: it was a basket.

"Ta-da! We thought you could use some cheering up."

"Who is 'we'?" I wanted to know, as I gazed down at the offerings.

"Me, Taylor, and a few others. We have some donuts, muffins, and other assorted goodies in there for you."

Taylor Adams was one of Jillian's best friends and, quite deservedly, the best baker in town. Oooo, I was gonna have fun with this basket. My thoughts trailed off as I stooped to slide a paperback novel out from under a blueberry muffin. The novel had a shirtless guy with a sword strapped to his back. The girl, who was barely wearing anything, gazed adoringly up at the muscular protagonist with something akin to hunger in her eyes. Questioningly, I looked over at my fiancée and attempted to raise a single eyebrow, in proper Vulcan fashion.

"Clara wanted to help," Jillian explained, as she fought to suppress a smile. "I tried to tell her you enjoy thrillers and good mystery novels, but no. She insisted we include this one."

Septuagenarian Clara Hanson owned and operated A Lazy Afternoon. Love the books she offers, but man alive, does she give me the creeps. No respect for your personal space, skin-tight clothes, and the libido of a teenager. That was why I typically headed in the opposite direction when I saw her coming.

"Why in the world would I ... holy cow. I still have the reporter on hold! I wanted to talk to you about those remains, too. Vance thinks he knows who they belong to."

Jillian frowned. "Reporters. I can't say I care too much for them. I can't abide rude people. They have to be the rudest people I have ever met."

"Ordinarily, I'd agree. However, this one is nothing of the sort. Calm, polite, and believe it or not, respectful."

"Are you sure she's a reporter?" Jillian teased. "Haven't I told you to tell your girlfriends not to call here whenever I'm around?"

I laughed, gave her a kiss, and returned to the call. While Jillian waited for me in the living room stroking Sherlock and Watson's luxurious fur, I stepped into the closest room, which happened to be the laundry room, and answered the reporter's questions as best as I could.

"That land hasn't been part of Lentari Cellars for very long. What's that? How long? Oh, I don't know. Since last year? That's right. I purchased that land from a neighboring farmer."

"Is everything okay?" Jillian mouthed, appearing in the doorway.

I smiled at her and nodded.

"What news station is she from?" Jillian asked.

For some reason, I covered the phone with my hand, thinking I was holding an old-fashioned telephone receiver, and that alone would mute the conversation. For heaven's sake, I had just used the mute button a few minutes ago. "She's from Arizona, from the main Phoenix newspaper."

"Do me a favor," Jillian softly implored. "Don't tell them who you bought the land from. As a courtesy, I'd try to give them a call first."

Nodding, I returned my attention to the call and answered another dozen or so questions before a notion dawned. Politely waiting for Kara to take a breath, I decided to ask the next question.

"Ms. Averson, let me ask you something."

"Of course. Go ahead."

"My cell phone showed the number you're calling from as having a local area code. Sure, the prefix wasn't recognized, but I do know for a fact your number—and mine—is an Oregon number. Care to explain that?"

"Oh, that. Believe it or not, that's a computer program. Don't tell anyone I told you this, but our phone system has the ability to mask our true phone number and, instead, display what we assume is a local number."

"Which results in more people being willing to answer the phone," I guessed.

"That's right. I'm sorry for the deception."

"Ms. Averson, don't be. You have to be the nicest reporter I've ever talked to. If you give me your direct number, then I'll be sure to pass along any new developments."

Kara thanked me profusely and then hung up.

"It's been five days since the Daredevils disbanded," I complained. "Just when I thought those phone calls were tapering off, now this happens. I've already explained to everyone who'd listen that I had no idea human remains were under those rocks. Now, everyone wants to find out what my connection is to Charles Hanson."

Jillian looked up, surprised. "Charles Hanson? You're kidding. That's who the bones belong to? Charlie Hanson?"

I gazed at my fiancée with a wee bit of skepticism evident on my face.

"You can't possibly tell me you know him. He's before our time."

"Of course he was, you silly man. However, his murder was big news back then. Every school child knew the story. After all, quite a bit of history is involved."

"History?" I scoffed. "Pertaining to a murder?"

"It's rumored Charles Hanson's murder is tied to the start of the Oregon Gold Rush."

"I've heard of the California Gold Rush," I admitted, "but not the Oregon one. Are you telling me that the Oregon Gold Rush started around 1968? I find that hard to believe."

"I don't remember the specifics," Jillian admitted, "but I know he was searching for something which would make him a lot of money."

I held up my hands in a time-out gesture. "Whoa. Wait a minute. Charlie Hanson gets himself killed, is somehow tied to this state's gold rush, and you say he was searching for something that'd make him wealthy."

Jillian nodded. "That's right. I wonder what Clara thinks about all of this."

"Why would she know anything about it?" I asked. "Hanson. Hmm. Is Charlie a relative?"

"I'm quite certain he is," Jillian decided.

"Did she say anything about the bones when you saw her?" I wanted to know.

Jillian patted the basket. "At the time this was assembled, none of us knew who those bones belonged to, so no, Clara hasn't said anything about it."

"Nothing's been confirmed," I reminded her. "They very well might belong to someone else. Level with me. If those bones are Charlie Hanson, how big of a news story would that be?"

"Huge," Jillian confirmed. "Let me ask you something. Do you remember who you bought that land from?"

I nodded. "Of course. That land was once part of Parson Farms, making Tim Parson the previous owner. However, I pretty much dealt with Jason, his son. He's the one who cut me a deal."

"Tim Parson," Jillian thoughtfully repeated. "He's an honest, hard-working farmer. There's no way he's involved with any wrong-doing."

"He *was* a farmer," I corrected. "By now, he's living it up in Florida, enjoying his retirement."

"Where's his son, Jason?" Jillian wanted to know.

I shrugged. "I really don't know. I don't think they live in town any more. I saw a for sale sign up on the house late last year. I'm pretty sure it sold, 'cause I haven't seen that sign in a while."

"All anyone would have to do is research the bill of sale and they'll see for themselves who last owned the property."

"They've probably already done so," I mused. "And if they haven't, then I'm sure the police have."

As I mentioned earlier, a lot has happened in the past two days. I've been interviewed dozens of times, had my official police consultant status revoked, reversed, and then revoked again. Chief Nelson told me that, for once, he knows I had nothing to do with what had happened to these remains, seeing how he places the age of the bones around fifty years or later. I'm pretty sure the chief was the one who started the rumor about the bones belonging to Charles Hanson. But, thanks to my history with this town, rumors started spreading and, just like that, I had people whispering about me behind my back.

Again.

At least this time, I knew that the majority of the people here in PV believed I wasn't involved in any illegal activities. Sure, those bones had to belong to someone, but until a DNA analysis could be done, or else the dental records came back with a match, I was going to remain a person of suspicion. I just had to prove that I had no connection to Charlie Hanson, or whomever the bones were confirmed to be.

As luck would have it, dental records identified the remains three hours later. The police department had been right. The bones belonged to one Charles S. Hanson. And, I get to add, Jillian was correct in that Charles was related to Clara. Turns out Charles Hanson, or Charlie, as he was known, was Clara Hanson's father.

How Jillian hadn't known that juicy piece of town gossip was beyond me. She seemingly knew everything about everyone. However, judging from the look on her face when Vance announced the identity, I'd say it had completely caught her unaware. According to the police report, Charlie Hanson disappeared over fifty years ago. Everyone knew he had been murdered, seeing how the scene of the crime had been located, and anyone who lost that much blood would never have survived. However, the body had never been discovered. That is, until Yours Truly dug him up from under a huge slab of rock.

Personally, I wanted to know how he got under there in the first place. Had someone tunneled under the stone and buried the body that way? Forensic investigators had thoroughly excavated the surrounding area where Mr. Hanson had been discovered. Thankfully—for me—every last piece of Charlie's skeleton had been located and recovered, meaning there shouldn't be any more surprises waiting for me out there under the ground.

My cell phone rang again. Once more, the display showed a local area code with an unknown prefix. Now that I knew the caller ID information could be faked, I set my phone to vibrate and put it on the coffee table. After a few moments, I rubbed my temples and groaned.

"I really don't need this right now."

Jillian took my hand and held it tight. "I know you don't. You, of all people, don't deserve this. However, that's not going to make the calls stop."

"What do you suggest?"

Jillian pulled out her phone and started tapping the screen.

"Well, first, I say we order dinner. How does pizza sound? From Sara's Pizza Parlor?"

My stomach chose that time to grumble.

"I'll take that as a yes," Jillian laughed, as she placed the order online. "And then, I think we should look into the circumstances of poor Charles' disappearance."

"You want us to take the case?" I hesitantly asked. "My status as a police consultant is currently on hold. I don't think I'd be welcome around the station, and I don't want to press my luck."

"Then don't go to the station. Your two best investigators are curled up right over there. And, you have me. I'm not as good at finding clues as either Sherlock or Watson, but I can certainly make myself useful. What do you say?"

An hour later, discarded paper plates sat forgotten on my coffee table. Both dogs had eaten their own dinners and were now out cold on the couch next to us. As for us, well, both Jillian and I had become completely immersed in 19th century Oregon history.

According to preliminary research, this area, meaning Pomme Valley and the surrounding area, had a very sizeable role in the start of the Oregon Gold Rush. Apparently, some guy, who only went by the name Red Dawg, had a very lucrative gold mine. According to multiple sources, Red Dawg would travel south for the winter into Northern California, and drop golden nuggets as payment for everything he purchased. Included in that list were drinks for everyone lucky enough to be in the tavern each night whenever he was there.

It was said that Red's mine wasn't in California but up north, here in Oregon. And, as luck would have it, that mine was rumored to be hidden somewhere in Pomme Valley itself. To say that jealous miners searched for it would be an understatement.

The two of us sat back on the couch, amazed. Could Charles Hanson have discovered the location of Red Dawg's hidden gold mine? Could there really be a hidden treasure somewhere in the area? Clearly, there had to be some truth to the stories, and the unfortunate Charles had uncovered something tangible. The problem was, whatever he found had led to his death.

THREE

D o you really think you can find him? I mean, the only thing we know is that he's somewhere in Florida."

"It shouldn't be too hard," I decided. "The name Tim Parson may not be the most unique of names, but I'm sure I can find him. I have to let him know what's going on here, before he's blindsided by the police."

Jillian gave me a warm smile. "That's very considerate of you. I wouldn't want the police to call me, out of the blue, and tell me human remains had been found on a piece of property I once owned, either. I will say that I'm interested to hear what he has to say about this whole mess."

Two hours later, I threw in the towel. I had searched for my former neighbor in public access databases, real estate sales, and even the SSDI—Social Security Death Index—all to no avail. Unless Farmer Parson had been abducted by aliens, then it would seem he had dropped off the face of the planet.

Jillian finally came to my rescue. I'm ashamed to admit it only took my lovely fiancée all of about five minutes to find him. It just goes to show you, it all depends on where you look.

"What was the name of his son?" Jillian had asked me, after I told her my search was coming up empty.

"The guy who originally made me the deal? Hmm, his name was Jason."

"Jason," Jillian softly repeated, as she typed away on her laptop. "And you're positive his father retired to Florida?"

"Yep. That's what I was told. I'm telling you; I've searched everywhere. I can't imagine what has happened to him. I'm even considering pulling up local newspaper websites to see if he's had some type of accident or heart attack, and has maybe passed away."

"I'm sure he's fine," Jillian said, as she continued to type.

"Good luck finding him. I don't think…"

"There he is."

I hurried to her side. "Excuse me?"

"Tim and Marie Parson, currently living in Ft. Lauderdale, Florida."

"How…? Where are you looking?"

Jillian spun her laptop around and tapped the screen. "Facebook, where else?"

I groaned. Social media. That one had escaped me. My publisher has been harassing me for months to build up my online presence on all those new social media sites, but I haven't ever done anything about it. I spend enough time tinkering around on a computer. Sharing my personal life with the world was not something that appealed to me in the slightest.

"I never would have called that," I admitted. "A retired farmer? On Facebook? What's this world coming to?"

Jillian laughed. "Actually, I didn't find Tim, but his son, Jason. He's younger, around our age. He has an account and less than an hour ago posted a picture of his family, lounging on the beach with the ocean as his backdrop."

"So, Jason is probably visiting his parents," I said, nodding. "That's good timing for us. Are you sure the father is nearby?"

Jillian tapped the screen. "I'd say so. I've only talked to him a few times, but I do remember what he looks like. That's him, standing in the background, holding a cocktail."

I looked for myself. Sure enough, there was Tim Parson, tanner than I remember, and a little heavier. There was someone who was enjoying his retirement, I decided. Jillian sent off a private message to Jason and then leaned back in her chair.

"Now we wait."

The wait only lasted thirty minutes. The two of us were sitting at the table, in the side room I called the Breakfast Nook, when Jillian's laptop started ringing like a telephone. Surprised, I looked over and she smiled at me.

"I told him to call me at his earliest convenience."

"On the computer?" I asked, dumbfounded.

"Facebook has the ability to allow video calls. Okay, sit here. Are you ready?" Jillian clicked on Receive and then stepped out of the picture.

The laptop's screen went dark and then, just as quickly, lit up, showing me a very tropical scene. A young man, whom I was guessing was in his late forties, was sitting at a bar, sipping a beer. He looked over at me and grinned.

"Mr. Anderson! It's good to see you!"

It was Jason, Tim's son.

"Hey there, Jason! Looks like you're having the time of your life."

"I am. I am seriously considering retiring here in a few years. The beaches are amazing."

"I've been to Fort Lauderdale a few times," I admitted. "It's nice there."

"I'm surprised to see you. I got a message from Jillian Cooper, asking me to call."

Jillian stepped into the frame.

"Hello. You must be Jason. I'm Jillian. It's nice to meet you."

"I remember you," Jason said, as he sipped his beer. "The cookbook store, right? My wife loved your store. She's already mentioned to me that she hopes she can find a similar store here, for when we eventually move here."

Jillian leaned forward and encompassed me in

a hug, from behind.

"Zachary is my fiancé. He was having some trouble locating your father, so I did a search through Facebook. I'm glad we found you."

"What's going on?" Jason asked, growing cautious. "Is everything okay?"

"Is your dad nearby?" I asked. "I need to let you guys know about something that was discovered on the land you sold me last year."

Jason nodded. "Well, if you're talking about oil, I'll give you my PayPal account. You can use that to deposit any amount you see fit to send our way."

I snorted with laughter while Jason grinned at me. My face quickly sobered, which caused Jason to frown.

"It's something more serious than that, isn't it?"

I nodded once. Jason looked off camera and let out a piercing whistle.

"Valerie? Could you get Dad for me? There's something he needs to hear."

A few minutes later, Tim appeared on screen, next to his son.

"Zack! Hey, there! What's going on? Is everything okay?"

"Hi, Tim. It's good to see you. Listen, before I say anything, are you in a location where I can give you some news?"

Tim shared an anxious look with his son before he sighed. "Good or bad?"

"Surprising," I answered.

Both father and son looked off camera, then checked to see who was behind them. For the record, no one else was in the frame other than them.

"We're pretty secluded here," Jason told me. "What's going on?"

"Human remains were found on the land you guys sold me," I reported. "I wanted to let you know before the local police here manage to track you down."

"Human remains?" Jason repeated, shocked. He looked at his father, whose shocked expression mirrored his own. "Good God, do you know who they belonged to?"

I nodded. "The remains were identified last night. They belong to a man named Charles Hanson."

Tim choked on his drink. Jason turned to give him a speculative look. "Dad, you've heard of him? Do you know who that is?"

"My father talked about his disappearance years and years ago," Tim confirmed. "He was friends with him. According to him, everyone was. Charlie's disappearance was all anyone could talk about for months."

"Do you have any idea who might have done it?" Jillian asked.

Tim shook his head. "My father said Charlie was well-liked by everyone. I have no idea who would have wanted to do that to the poor guy.

You're serious, Zack? They know for certain it was ol' Charlie Hanson?"

"Confirmed through dental records."

"That's terrible," Jason said, as he sighed. He fixed me with a stare. "You don't think we had anything to do with it, do you?"

I shook my head. "Honestly? It's never crossed my mind. But, I wanted to give you a heads-up about it before you're blindsided by the PV police."

Tim gravely nodded. "Thank you, Zack. I appreciate you telling us. You're right. That's the last thing I'd expect to hear, coming from PV. We'll be waiting to hear from them."

"You're welcome. I wish we could have been doing this under better circumstances."

Father and son nodded, smiled politely, and then signed off.

"Do you think Tim was telling the truth?" I asked, as I turned to Jillian.

"I do. I was watching his face the entire time. He was just as surprised as we had been, upon learning who had been buried on his former property. He didn't have anything to do with it."

"Where does that leave us?" I inquired.

A smile formed on her face. "Well, I have an idea what to do next, only I can guarantee you're not going to like it."

"Psssht. Hit me with your best, lady. Let's see what you got."

Thirty minutes later, I was sulking like a petulant child.

"Have I not gone on record, multiple times, in saying I don't really care for her?" I explained, throwing every ounce of whine I could muster into my protest.

"Stop your fretting," Jillian told me, as she stepped out of my Jeep. She set the dogs on the ground, wrapped their leashes around her hand, and then turned expectantly to me. "She might have some useful information for us. Are you coming?"

I refused to budge.

"Come on, Zachary. She's really not that bad. I know you couldn't possibly be afraid of a little old lady, could you?"

My hands still hadn't left the wheel.

"Suit yourself. We're going inside. Just wait until I start spreading the rumor that the great Zachary Anderson is afraid of women in their seventies. What will the town think? My goodness, I can't wait to see what everyone says. I'm glad I brought my phone with me."

"You have a mean streak, lady," I grumbled, as I unbuckled my seat belt and stepped out of my Jeep. "I don't recall you being this mean before."

Jillian batted her eyes at me and blew me a kiss.

I approached the door of A Lazy Afternoon and couldn't hide the groan that escaped my lips. Of all the places I wanted to be today, this was nowhere on the list.

It had been Jillian's suggestion to see if Clara

would be willing to talk to us about her father. After all, based on her age and the year her father had died, she would have been in her early twenties when her father disappeared. Surely, she should be able to remember what he had been working on, shouldn't she?

We heard a chime as the door opened. Both dogs stepped inside first, followed immediately by Jillian. Sighing, I crossed over the threshold, into Clara's bookstore, and immediately came to a stop. I didn't see her, and I may not have been able to hear her, but I knew she was close.

"Hi, Ruby. How are you today?"

There was a mad fluttering of wings and, moments later, I felt two little claws grip my shoulder. A small African gray parrot had appeared on my shoulder and immediately nuzzled the side of my face. For some reason, and I'm still unclear why, Ruby the parrot has taken to me, and insists on riding my shoulder whenever I'm in the store. I used to think it was a ploy from Clara, which would allow her to get way too close to me in order to reclaim her bird. However, the look of amazement on Clara's face every time her bird favored me over her continued to amuse me and frustrate her.

"Ruby? Get back here, you crazy bird!"

Clara Hanson appeared from behind one of her racks of books. This time, her hair was down, but braided into a long rope which fell down her back. And, for the record, her hair was still the same color as the last time I had seen it, which was cotton-candy pink.

"Zack, darling! So good of you to pay me a visit!"

"We're all here," I clarified, as I stepped up to Jillian's side.

"I can see that," Clara said, as she nodded her head. "What brings you to my fine establishment today? Are you here to take me for a drive in that wonderful car of yours?"

I sadly shook my head and pointed outside. "I've got the Jeep today, I'm afraid. Hey, listen, are you busy? Could we talk to you?"

"I will always make time for you, darlin'!" Clara crooned. She sidled up next to me and sighed wistfully. "What can I help you with today, lover-boy?"

I looked over at Jillian. We both knew this was more than likely going to be a touchy subject. Thankfully, she had already volunteered to be the bearer of bad news.

"Clara," Jillian slowly began, "I don't suppose you've heard about the human remains discovered at Zachary's winery, have you?"

Clara nodded. "Of course, of course. Who hasn't? It's the talk of the town, isn't it? There's nothing like a good round of gossip to help you feel alive!"

I nervously cleared my throat. "Er, have you heard that the remains have been identified?"

Clara's mouth snapped closed and she shook

her head. "This must be hot off the press, honey. Usually, I'd get someone in here telling me the latest. Well, don't stop now. I'm dyin' to know, darlin'. Who is it?"

"Charles S. Hanson," Jillian quietly answered.

Clara's face drained of color. Her hands started to shake and darned if it didn't look like she was ready to collapse. Jillian hurriedly fetched the stool behind the counter and slid it under her.

"Just sit down, Clara. Deep breaths. How are you doing?"

"The bones on your property," Clara tremulously began, "they're my father? What ... h-how do you know? Uh, are ... are you sure?"

"They're sure," Jillian confirmed, using as gentle a voice as she could. "Dental records say there could be no mistake. Your father was found on Zachary's property."

Clara turned to point back at the counter where her cash register was sitting.

"C-could someone bring me a bottle of water? There's a small fridge under the counter right over there."

"I'll get it," I volunteered.

Sherlock and Watson both knew something was up. They crowded close to Clara and refused to leave her side. Clara, for her part, didn't even notice they were there.

"Here you go," I said, as I twisted off the bottle's top and handed it over.

"How was he found?" Clara finally asked, after

sitting in silence for a few moments.

I pointed at the dogs. "Sherlock and Watson deserve the honors. I was in my tractor, trying to clear some land, when both dogs wanted outside. Sherlock started to dig, and that's when he, er, found the remains."

"He was found on your land," Clara softly repeated.

"Actually, Lentari Cellars hasn't owned that land for long," I gently pointed out.

Clara then practically leapt to her feet, which spooked both dogs. Sherlock fired off a couple of warning woofs, but then settled down.

"What in God's name was my father doing out in the middle of nowhere?" Clara demanded, growing angry. "Do you have any idea how many afternoons and weekends I spent putting up flyers? How many hours ... days I spent looking for him? Our home was in town, not out in the country. Someone had to have lured him out there. Someone had to have given him a reason to go."

"That's what we were hoping to talk to you about," Jillian said. "You obviously knew your father better than anyone. Do you remember much about the time he disappeared?"

"Do I remember much?" Clara asked, appalled. "Honey, of course I do. He was my father, and I was in my twenties. Twenty-two, to be exact. The year was 1968, and I can remember that day as clear as the day I landed my first husband."

"I'm not sure how to respond to that," I quietly

whispered into Jillian's ear.

"Shush," she scolded, and turned to Clara. "We'd love to learn more about him. Whatever you can tell us would be helpful."

Clara sighed and drained nearly half her bottle of water, which I thought was impressive. Don't ask me why. A wistful look came over her features and, for the first time ever, I heard Ms. Clara Hanson speak and act like a normal person.

"My father was the kindest man you'd ever lay eyes on," the bookstore owner began. "He'd be the first to greet you as you walked into a room, and he'd be the last person to leave a party. Daddy had a heart of gold. No one could find a bad thing to say about him. Ever."

I came up, behind Jillian, and wrapped my arms around her. Together, we listened to Clara recall memories of her father. Sherlock and Watson, already snuggled up next to Clara, laid their heads down and promptly went to sleep. Ruby, who was still on my shoulder, bobbed her head a few times as she studied her owner. After a few moments, the little gray parrot flew to Clara's shoulder and snuggled close. Without turning her head, Clara reached up to stroke the feathers on the side of Ruby's head, a gesture she must have done often because the parrot closed her eyes and cooed softly.

"What you need to understand about my father," Clara continued, "was that he was always looking for the next get-rich-quick scheme. It infuriated my mother to no end."

"Can you remember any of them?" Jillian gently asked.

"Remember what?" Clara wanted to know. "Oh. You're asking about some of his whack-job schemes? Well, let's see. There was the time he invested $500 in a new shrimping outfit."

"What's so risky about that?" I curiously asked.

"If you know what you're doing, you can make a great living off of the shrimp that live out there," Clara informed us. "For example, did you know that shrimp are light-sensitive? They typically reside in water two to five hundred feet deep. At night, they head to shallow water to feed."

"You know your shrimp," Jillian decided, as she smiled at Clara.

"My second husband was a fisherman," Clara casually informed us. "I learned more about the fishing out there than I ever wanted to know. The numbskulls who conned Daddy out of his money had a tiny boat, no real gear, but they spun a vivid tale of great wealth. Naturally, my father fell for it."

"How often would he do something like that?" Jillian asked.

"My father, while being the most loving dad a girl could ask for, wasn't the sharpest tool in the shed."

I let out a laugh, but catching the frown Jillian threw me, quickly slapped a hand over my face. Glancing at Clara, I could see she never even noticed I had laughed at her. Clara, completely ignoring me, focused her attention on Jillian.

"Daddy had a gambling problem," Clara quietly said. "He just wasn't able to save any money. If fortune smiled on him, and he was given ten dollars, he'd find a way to lose nine of it. He was always looking for money, which I figured fueled his passion for his crazy schemes."

Ruby chose that time to fly down from Clara's shoulder and alight on Sherlock's back. The feisty corgi cracked an eye and regarded the intruder for a few moments before he surprised me by going to back to sleep. Jillian nudged me and pointedly looked down at the dogs. I gave her a thumbs up, indicating I had witnessed the phenomenon and was unsure what to do next. Ruby, in the meantime, hopped up to Sherlock's scruff, fluttered about for a bit, and then—much to everyone's surprise—nestled down into the corgi's soft fur.

Clara blinked a few times as she stared at her parrot before shrugging.

"What did your father do for a living?" I eventually asked. I've always been uncomfortable around silence, and since both Jillian and Clara were watching Ruby, I felt it was up to me to keep the conversation going. "Did he have a profession?"

"I don't really have an answer for that," Clara sighed. "Plumber? Painter? Stock broker? Daddy tried it all. He was always changing jobs. The ship was always docked in another port."

"Ship?" I repeated, confused. "What ship?"

"I'm thinking she's referring to the proverbial saying," Jillian answered, drawing a nod from Clara. "You know, 'when my ship comes in…'?"

"Exactly," Clara confirmed, "only it never did."

"What's the last thing you remember about your father?" I asked.

Clara shrugged and closed her eyes. After a few minutes of silence, which had me and Jillian nervously eyeing each other, Clara took a deep breath.

"I remember telling him I was going out with a boy. Coincidentally, it was Darrel, who ended up being my first husband, but we wouldn't get married for a few years. Anyway, I remember my father acting excited. He said he was on to something."

Jillian and I straightened. This was what we wanted to hear.

"He said his ship had finally come in and that the project he was working on would solve all our financial worries. Overnight."

"Did you ever ask him what that was?" Jillian wanted to know.

Clara shook her head. "I wanted to, but never got the chance. I had planned on cornering him the following morning, which would have been Saturday, and asking him what he was talking about. With mama gone, it was up to me to make all the important decisions. So, Daddy usually ran things by me first, to see what my opinion was, before he actually did anything."

"And you never got the chance," I deduced.

Clara sadly nodded.

"If you don't mind me saying this," I hesitantly began, "have you ever known him to be working on anything illegal?"

Clara let out a short bark of laughter. "With Daddy, I can almost guarantee he had his fingers in the wrong pot. If it had the possibility of making a buck, then he'd be more than willing to look the other way."

"I thought you said he ran things by you first?" I argued.

"He did," Clara said, nodding. "At least, he *usually* did. If he knew the scheme was illegal, yet it had the chance to bring in a lot of money, then he'd wait until he had something to show for his effort before confronting me."

Satisfied, I nodded. Figuring our interview was over, I prepared to wake the dogs, only Clara had one more surprise waiting for us. She fixed us with a frank stare and smiled. Not creepily, mind you, but a genuine, caring smile.

"You want to know about it, don't you?"

"Do we want to know about what?" Jillian curiously asked.

"The mine, of course."

My eyebrows shot up. "You wouldn't be referring to an infamous missing mine, would you?"

Clara grinned again. "Dawg's Lost Cabin Gold Mine. So, you have heard of it."

I looked at my watch and nodded. "I have, as a matter of fact. I learned about it twelve hours ago."

It was Clara's turn to look surprised. "Really?"

Jillian patted my arm. "Remember, Zachary only moved here a few years ago."

"Of course. I should have thought of that. So, Zackie-boy, what do you know about that mine?"

"What do you know about that mine?" I countered.

"Only that Red Dawg himself was single-handedly responsible for the start of the Oregon Gold Rush."

"Was his name really Red Dawg?" I asked, perplexed. "What kind of a messed up name is that?"

"No one really knew his true identity," Clara confirmed. "Many people speculated, but nothing ever came of it. The only thing they knew was that Red Dawg was a redhead, he had a mine somewhere along Rascal River, and that he trekked between Southwestern Oregon and Northern California every winter."

"What part of California?" I asked.

"Yreka," Clara answered.

"From the brief bit of research we've done," I began, "we've learned that quite a few people have ended up looking for that mine."

"That's right, sugar."

Great. Clara was starting to sound more and more like her old self. I know that was for the best, for Clara. As for me, however, I was back to suppressing my full-body shudders.

"That's how the Oregon Gold Rush started," Clara explained. "You see, you have to understand what Red Dawg did every night he was in town, in Yreka."

Caught up in Clara's narrative, I eagerly leaned forward. "What? What'd he do?"

"He strolled right up to his favorite tavern, plunked down several gold nuggets, and bought drinks for everyone in the house."

"Generous," Jillian decided.

I frowned and shook my head. "Stupid."

Surprised, Jillian swatted my arm. "Zachary, that was a mean thing to say. If someone bought drinks for everyone in the house, every single night, would that not be construed as generous?"

"Stupid and foolish," I argued. "Look, let's think about this. What happens if you waltz into a tavern, loaded with gold, and show everyone in the place that you've clearly struck it rich? What do you think is gonna happen to you?"

Jillian's eyes widened. "Oh. I hadn't considered that. You're right. It'd be foolish to flaunt your wealth."

"Especially in that time period," Clara agreed. "Since every hooligan you can think of frequented those taverns at night, you can only imagine how much interest he generated."

"Probably quite a bit," I surmised. "Did anyone ever get the location of the mine out of him?"

"People followed him for years, in an attempt

to track him back to his mine. Now, whether or not anyone was ever successful remains to be seen. There's a handful of local folk tales which feature a lost gold mine. I personally think it's safe to say they're referencing Red Dawg's mine, which means nobody has ever found it."

"Crazy," I decided. "I wonder if any of these folk tales have been studied? Maybe there are clues to its location?"

Clara nodded. "Honey, there have been college courses which have focused on deciphering the location of that mine. Others have tried recreating the route which Dawg would have taken, from Yreka to Southwestern Oregon, or the other way 'round."

"Wow," I mouthed to Jillian, who nodded.

"Then there are those who believe Dawg was ambushed by Indians. Others say a few unscrupulous fellows finally caught up with him and killed him. The only thing anyone can agree on was that Red Dawg stopped making his annual pilgrimages back to California."

"Something had to have happened to him," I decided.

"Do you think it's true?" Jillian asked Clara. "Do you think Red Dawg's lost gold mine is real?"

"Oh, honey," Clara exclaimed, "not only is it real, it's in PV."

"How can you be so sure?" I asked.

"Because I'm fairly certain my father knew something about that mine, and that is what got him killed."

FOUR

H e found it," I exclaimed. "He had to have found where Red Dawg hid his mine. It's the only thing that makes sense."

"There are a number of other possibilities," Jillian hastily said. "Charlie's death could just be bad luck. He…"

"Bad luck?" I repeated. "Being killed and buried on someone else's property is a little more serious than simple bad luck, don't you think?"

Jillian shrugged. "It could be. I'm just saying we don't have any concrete proof Clara's father located the missing mine."

Clara frowned and swept an arm around her bookstore. "Do you see my father anywhere? Did you not hear me tell you that he was loved by everyone in town? My father has been dead for over fifty years. The only way anyone would want to kill him would be if he had stumbled into some money. Lots of money. Like a gold mine? Hmm? Hmm?"

Jillian and I shared a look together.

"The simple fact that he's not here is your proof," Clara insisted.

Jillian squeezed my hand the moment I took a breath. I didn't have to look at her. She was warning me to keep my big trap shut, which I just realized I was more than happy to do. Giving Clara what I hoped was a supportive smile, we thanked her for her time and ushered the dogs to the door. Ruby, who had fallen asleep on Sherlock's back, seemed content to use the tri-colored corgi as her own personal steed. It wasn't until we reached the door that I remembered the little parrot was nestled on Sherlock's back. Curious to see if she was still there, I leaned down for a closer look.

"You still have your hitchhiker, pal," I told Sherlock. "We can't go outside until she flies off."

Clara came hurrying up to us, flashed us an apologetic look, and snatched her bird off of Sherlock's back. Unfortunately, Ruby didn't care one bit for being removed from her warm, makeshift nest. She squawked irritably and tried to cling to Sherlock's fur, which resulted in several tufts of black fur appearing in Ruby's talons.

"I am so sorry," Clara said, horrified. She gave Ruby a scathing look and immediately ruffled Sherlock's fur. "I'm so sorry, boy. She didn't hurt you, did she?"

Sherlock bent around to look at Watson, who immediately approached her packmate's back and inspected it for herself. After a few moments, she snorted and returned her attention to the door. Satisfied everything was in order, Sherlock tugged at his leash, showing me he was anxious to go.

We had just made a right, on Oregon St. and were picking up speed, when I noticed we were approaching Pomme Valley Mercantile, which was a small, hardware-type store. Remembering I had knocked Jillian's screen door clean off its tracks after thinking the thing was already open, and broke one of the cheap, plastic wheels, I pulled over.

"Well, we made it far," Jillian wryly observed. "What did we stop here for? Do you need something at the hardware store?"

"I told you I'd fix your screen door," I reminded her. "I need to pick up another wheel or two."

Jillian let out a giggle. "In preparation for next time, huh? This makes the third time you've walked into that screen door. Perhaps it's time for an eye exam?"

"Hardy har har. No, I'll be fine. I don't suppose you'd like to come in with me?"

"Into a hardware store? Why, I'd be delighted."

"You would? I'm surprised. You don't really strike me as a DIY type of person."

"I'm not," Jillian confided, as she stepped out of the car and set Watson on the ground. "But you are, so that means the possibilities are endless. Besides, I always enjoy looking at things and getting ideas."

Hand in hand, the two of us led the dogs past The Toy Shoppe, which was Spencer Woodson's store. We caught sight of Zoe and her father, sitting together behind the counter, and waved at them. Both waved back.

"I really enjoy small towns," I murmured, as I held open the door allowing Jillian and the dogs to enter the hardware store. "I never thought I'd hear myself say that as often as I have."

I took Sherlock's leash, and with Jillian holding onto Watson's, we began perusing the aisles.

"Is there anything you'd like to look at?" I companionably asked, as we stopped to look at the latest selection of twelve by twelve inch travertine tile.

"Why don't you get what you need first," Jillian suggested. "Then, we can look around. Hmm, I do need to get a new ceiling fan for Highland House. The one in the game room isn't nearly big enough. I can barely feel any air movement when it's on, even if I have it on full strength."

"One big ceiling fan," I noted. "Got it."

Who would've thought there'd be so many choices for screen door hardware? I had left Jillian and the dogs looking at new washers and dryers while I wandered the aisles, looking for related hardware. Once I found it, though, a new problem presented itself. There must've been a dozen different types and styles of screen door wheels. One glance told me that it wasn't one size fits all. Heck, it wasn't even one size fits most.

One wheel was metal and encased in a rectangular plastic housing. Another looked as though the wheel was mounted on the end of a large spring, and was designed to be shoved up inside the door frame. How was I supposed to know which one I needed? I was going to need help, and that's when the second problem became apparent. There was no one to ask for help. This was a small store, so it shouldn't have been too difficult to spot someone roaming the aisles, but darned if I could find anyone.

Grumbling to myself, I back-tracked to the front of the store and found the clerk. I told him what I needed, and he promptly directed me to the aisle I had already found. Swallowing my anger, I again told him what I needed, and then added I wasn't too sure what style I needed, nor could I identify the door's manufacturer.

"If you don't remember, then I'm not going to be able to do much for you," the clerk advised, shrugging helplessly. "That is, unless you'd like to buy one of each kind and then return the rest."

"Maybe," I groaned. "I really should have brought the broken wheel with me."

"Okay, let's try this," the clerk said. I had to give him credit. At least he was trying to find a way to help me. "How old is the door?"

"The old screen door? Hoo boy. Maybe thirty years? It's an oldie, no doubt about it."

"You have a thirty-year-old screen door?" the clerk incredulously repeated. "Wow. In that case,

I don't think there's anything here that would be compatible."

"What do you recommend?" I asked, exasperated.

"A new door?" the clerk sarcastically suggested.

"But, all it needs are wheels!"

"Which you can no longer get," the clerk reminded me.

"Fine," I grumbled. "I'll take a new door. Oh, well. It's only money, right? Could you bring it up here for me? I have to go find my fiancée."

"Is she the one walking around with the two cute dogs?"

I nodded. "That's her. She's probably looking at ceiling fans. Which direction are those?"

"Ceiling fans are that way," the clerk said, pointing left. "Pretty much the opposite corner of the store."

"Perfect. Thanks."

"Only..."

I froze, mid-step.

"...she's no longer at the ceiling fans."

"Uh-huh. Where is she now?"

The clerk glanced under the counter, which I'm guessing was where some small security monitors could be found. "Over there, on your right. She's headed for the outdoor section."

"Flowers," I chuckled. "Should've called that one. Thanks."

I found Jillian admiring a half-whiskey-barrel

display full of bright, colorful flowers. Coming up behind her, I stopped to inspect the floral display before us. Petunias, if memory serves. Purple, orange, and red specimens were arranged in layers, which encircled the open whiskey barrel. I could see several thin, black tubes snaking up and into the barrel, which would, no doubt, provide automatic watering.

The dogs, on the other hand, were both staring up at a rack of aromatic plants in individual colorful cups. According to a nearby sign, they were young herb plants. And, judging from the basket Jillian was now holding, she had noticed the rack and already made several selections.

Without turning around, and without giving any signs she knew I was standing behind her, Jillian held out her basket and waited for me to take it.

"How many times have I told you not to do that?" I chuckled, as I took the proffered basket. "It's creepy."

"You're a heavy breather," Jillian said, as she slowly turned to give me a backward glance. She blew me a kiss and handed me both dogs' leashes. "Would you mind? I see some plants ahead that warrant a second look."

Nodding, I took the leashes and started to pull the dogs away from the plant display stand. However, neither dog budged. I felt the leashes go taut and automatically glanced back to see why. Both corgis were still staring at the rack of herbs.

"They're plants," I told the dogs. "Let them be. Come on. We're gonna follow Jillian."

No response.

"Guys? What, did I not give you your treats this morning? What's wrong with you two?"

Sherlock finally looked over at me, whined, and then returned his attention to the herbs.

"If you're that interested, then let me put you at ease. Jillian picked some of these up, ok? Now, let's go."

Still no dice. Grumbling, I pulled out my cell, and had no sooner snapped a few pictures when both dogs rose to their feet and trotted off, as though they had lost interest.

"Dogs."

Spoke too soon. We only made it about ten feet down the aisle when the dogs hit the brakes again. This time, there were no plants to ogle, only row after row of seeds on a small, spinning display stand. Curious, I leaned forward to see what they were. This particular side of the display had vegetables. I could see packets of seeds for carrots, lettuce, tomatoes, and cucumbers.

"Are you guys in the mood for a salad? Come on. Actually, hold on a sec. I know we won't make it far without a few snapshots."

Pictures taken, we made it to Jillian, who by this time, had somehow found a cart and was pushing it around. In it were several flats of a variety of flowers. She looked up at me and smiled.

"Perfect timing, Zachary. Do you think you

could load one of those whiskey barrels up onto this thing? I'd like to buy one. Well, maybe two, if you can get two of them to fit."

"I doubt very much you'd get one of those things in your cart without squishing your flowers flat. No, what you need is one of those flat-bed trolley things I've seen around here."

"Excellent. Would you fetch me one?"

I walked into that one. Handing the leashes to Jillian, I headed to the front of the store to get a bigger cart. Again, by the time I had returned, I discovered that Jillian had been busy. The cart was almost full. Topsoil, fertilizer, plant spikes, and so on had been added to the mix.

Chuckling, I added two half-whiskey barrels.

"I think you single-handedly keep this place in business," I joked. Then, after realizing that she very well could have a financial stake in this store, I sobered and offered her a sheepish smile. "Sorry. If you already do, then I apologize."

"Contrary to what you may think," Jillian teased, "I do not own the entire town, you silly man."

I returned the grin and pushed the trolley in behind Jillian.

"It's only about forty-five percent of the town."

Surprised, I turned back to my fiancée, who giggled as soon as she caught sight of my face.

"That was a joke, Zachary."

Chuckling, I returned my attention to my trolley, and the balancing act I was performing. The last thing I wanted to do was let these things topple over, so for me, progress to the cashier was slow. After a few minutes, and a quick conversation about Wi-Fi controlled light bulbs and their completely impractical use (according to Jillian), I noticed Jillian slow her cart and eventually stop. About ready to ask her what the holdup was, she turned to me and gave me an apologetic look.

"I'm sorry, Zachary."

"Huh? You're sorry? For what?"

"For what's about to happen. I have no idea how she knew you were here."

"Who are you talking about? What's going on?"

I leaned around Jillian to see for myself. That's when I saw an older woman who was wearing business attire and had her gray hair pulled back in a tight bun. She was pacing outside the store, clutching a thick manila envelope to her chest. As was typical with her, she was frowning.

Abigail Lawson.

Here was a person who truly, and I mean completely, hated my guts. I knew she was related to my late wife's side of the family, only I'm not sure how the two were related. What I do know, however, is that Abigail feels I single-handedly cheated her out of her inheritance. You see, her mother, Bonnie Davies, Lentari Cellars' previous owner, had made it clear to her daughter, Abigail, that she would never sell the winery, and had no intentions of letting her life's work become absorbed by some big-name corporation. Based on letters and correspondence I've found in photo albums back in Bonnie's old house (my current home), I know full well that Abigail had pestered her mother long and hard to give control of the winery to her, which would allow her to sell it off to the highest bidder.

But, as fortune would have it, once Bonnie died, she left her entire estate, which included the winery, to me and Samantha. Since Sam was deceased, that meant everything had suddenly become mine. Abigail tried to get me to 'do the right thing' and sign over everything to her, since (according to her), that was what her mother really wanted. However, I decided to keep the winery and reopen it, to honor my late wife.

Will Abigail let the matter drop? No. Has she tried several times to wrest control away from me? Yes. Will she continue to try? Indubitably. And … will I ever consider selling? Not a chance.

With that said, I groaned, looked over at the clerk, and pointed at the two carts.

"Will you help her with this? I need to step outside and ruin a grouchy old lady's day."

"We'll take care of her," the clerk assured me.

"Be cordial," Jillian instructed, as I gave her a quick peck on the cheek. "Keep your cool."

I took Watson's leash from Jillian and nodded. Stepping outside, into the bright sunshine, I saw Abigail pivot on her heel and face me. Right on cue, both dogs let off a warning growl as Abigail headed toward me, her heels clipping loudly on the sidewalk. She placed herself directly in front of me and fell silent.

"If you're waiting for me to say hello, then fine, I'll say it. Hello. And now, I'll throw in a 'have a good one.' Good bye."

"Mr. Anderson," Abigail called, as I turned around to head back into the store, "we have some business to discuss."

"No, we don't," I said, as I paused and glanced back at her. Abigail was once more wearing a set of her thick, bulbous sunglasses, giving her the appearance of a bug-eyed monster.

"Would you hear me out?" Abigail called, as I reined in the dogs and headed back inside. "Please."

That one word stopped me in my tracks. Plastering a guarded look on my face, I turned around again.

"Why should I?" I asked. When Abigail began sputtering, I pressed on. "You have never been cordial to me. You've never been polite. Quite the contrary, you've been downright ugly."

Abigail's lips thinned as she stared at me.

"So, tell me something," I continued. "Why should I be polite and cordial to you?"

Abigail hefted the large envelope she was holding. "Our history may have a few bumps," she hesitantly began, "but..."

"History?" I interrupted. "There is no history between us." I pointed at the envelope she was holding. "Once again, I'll say the following: if you're thinking I'm going to sell, based on some crackpot new idea, or proposal you've come up with, then the answer is no. Once and for all, will you please listen to me and let that sink in? Seriously, we can save each other a lot of time and headaches if you'll just accept that as fact. What do you say?"

"I'll say that I think you just need to hear me out."

Was it me or, for once, was Abigail sounding the slightest bit cordial? Since when had Queen Stuckup acted polite? She was up to something, and that scared the ever-lovin' crap out of me.

"I can see you're skeptical," Abigail continued, as she kept her voice calm and neutral. She opened the envelope she'd been holding and pulled out a wad of papers. "I think you'll want to see this."

I sighed and started walking toward my parked Jeep. Abigail didn't miss a beat, and fell into step beside me.

"Yes or no," I began, after a few moments of silence had passed. "Are you trying to get me to sell the winery?"

Abigail hesitated for a brief second and eventually nodded. "I am."

"Then, the answer is an automatic no," I told her, as I unlocked my Jeep and folded the two mid-row passenger seats down in anticipation of loading in the two large half-barrels. "I don't know how many times I can say this: I'm not interested in selling. End of story."

"You haven't read my offer," Abigail pointed out. Again, the accusatory tones she was normally accustomed to using were mysteriously absent. "I think this will sway your mind."

"Allow me to venture a guess. You're going to offer me even more money. The answer is still no."

"I'm aware Lentari Cellars recently won some awards at the San Francisco International Wine Competition, did it not?"

I nodded. "Caden won several medals. Two platinum, three gold, and a silver, if memory serves. What about them?"

"With those latest awards," Abigail continued, as she thrust the wad of papers at me once more, "I've managed to convince my investors to make you a seven-figure offer. It's all in there, Mr. Anderson. With the purchase of Lentari Cellars, I'll be creating a brand new board to oversee the day-to-day operations of the winery. You'll also note that you'll have a place on that board."

She really was grasping at straws. Trying to bribe me with my own winery? This was gutsy, Abigail, even for you. However, I wasn't gonna tell her that.

At that time, Jillian and two store clerks exited the hardware store and headed toward me. I lifted both corgis into the Jeep, leaned in through the open driver window to start the car, and then turned back to Abigail. I was about ready to tell her to mind her own business, and that the winery was mine, when a thought occurred. No, I had no intention of entertaining Abigail's offer, but based on recent events, a few questions had arisen. Perhaps I could get Abigail to answer some of them?

"Your cordiality surprises me," I ended up admitting, which had the effect of Jillian's head whipping over to stare incredulously at me. "I appreciate your calmness, and politeness. I'll tell you what I'll do. Ordinarily, your presence here would have typically earned you a resounding 'hell no' to whatever you were asking for."

Abigail's eyes narrowed, but she didn't say anything.

"I'll take this home and will take the time to read this. I will forewarn you that I'm 99.99 percent certain the answer will still be a no, seeing how I don't need the money, and I want to keep the winery open in my late wife's memory. Do you understand that?"

Abigail nodded. "I do. If you're willing to look at the proposal, then I can only hope you will be able to see the logic of my offer, and are willing to accept. Or, perhaps, counter-offer."

"Unlikely," I warned. "But, if I do this for you, you have to do something for me. Quid pro quo."

Abigail had just handed me the envelope and spun on her heel when she hesitated. With suspicion written all over her face, Abigail Lawson, sworn enemy of Yours Truly, turned back to me and put her hands on her hips. After a few moments, she sighed.

"What do you want, Mr. Anderson?"

"I want you to answer a few questions for me. Give me clear, honest answers, and I will read this thing through, cover to cover. Do we have a deal?"

"What do you want to know?" Abigail cautiously asked.

"Were you stalking me?" I turned to point at the hardware store. "How did you know I was in there?"

Abigail was silent as she shifted weight from leg to leg. I tapped the envelope I was holding and waggled a finger at her.

"A deal's a deal. If you want me to read this, then please answer the question. Truthfully."

"I know the owner of the store," Abigail hesitantly admitted. "He knew I was in town, and whenever I'm here, I pay well to know where certain people will be at all times."

"And I'm on that list," I guessed.

"You are the list," Abigail confirmed. "Is that all?"

"No. Is there a reason why you're here? In Pomme Valley, that is."

Abigail nodded and pointed at the envelope in my hands. "Of course. For that."

"You're here because you think I'm going to agree to one of your offers?"

"I can make you a millionaire," Abigail promised. "You'd be a fool to not accept."

"There's your first mistake," I said, as my voice lowered. "Never insult the people you're trying to negotiate with. It'll never end well."

Abigail sighed loudly and waged some type of internal war, because I saw her left eye twitch and her bottom lip tremble. "I a-apologize."

Holy crap on a cracker. It's official, sports fans. Hell hath officially frozen over. Abigail Lawson has apologized? If I wasn't creeped out before, then I sure was now. Glancing over at Jillian, and seeing the bemused expression on her face, I shook my head. But, before I could say anything else, Abigail fired off a question of her own.

"Why are you asking?"

"I just need to know if your presence here coincides with the discovery."

"The discovery?" Abigail repeated, as she frowned. "The discovery of what?"

"How well did you know the family who farmed the land to the northwest of the winery?" I asked, as I ignored her question.

Abigail blinked a few times as she struggled to find the angle she figured I had to be playing. "You want to know who owned the land northwest of the winery? I think that was a family by the name of Parson."

I nodded. "Correct. Did you know them well?"

Abigail shrugged. "No. Why do you ask?"

I watched Jillian approach my side and take my hand.

"Because human remains were found on that land," I quietly answered.

"What?" Abigail gasped. "Who was it, do you know?"

"I'll get to that in just a sec," I answered, as I studied Abigail's face. Thus far, I had to admit, it appeared Abigail hadn't known anything about the bones. All I could see was genuine shock. "That land was included in the parcel I purchased off of the Parson family."

"I know of the winery's expansion," Abigail announced. She looked at the envelope again. "That was one of the reasons we were able to increase the offer as substantially as we did."

"When was Lentari Cellars founded?" I asked, ignoring Abigail's attempt to steer the conversation back to her proposal.

Abigail blinked a few times. "I don't follow."

"When was the winery started?" I asked. "Who started it, your mother?"

Abigail nodded. "Yes. My mother planted her first vine when she was sixteen. She knew what she wanted to do with her life from the moment she was born. That's how dedicated she was."

"And that's probably why she never wanted to sell," Jillian added.

"Hmmph," Abigail scowled. "My mother was old. The day-to-day operations of a winery were taking their toll on her. She needed to retire."

"She had Caden running the winery," I reminded Abigail, but upon seeing her face darken with anger, I decided to refrain from provoking her any further. "Look, there's no need to stir anything up for now. The reason I ask is, back then, did you guys have any interaction with the Hanson family?"

"The Hanson family?" Abigail repeated, puzzled. "I thought we were talking about the Parson family. Hanson. Hmm. I do remember a family by that name. What about them?"

"Well, those remains I found? They belong to one Charles Hanson. He was Clara Hanson's father."

Abigail gasped, which had Jillian and me sharing a glance. Was Abigail acting, or was she genuinely upset?

"Charlie? Those remains were Charlie Hanson's?"

"You knew him?" Jillian asked.

Abigail nodded. "He disappeared over fifty years ago. What in the world was he doing on Parson land?"

"What do you remember of his disappearance?" I asked. Again, I acted like I hadn't heard her question. "Is there anything you can tell us?"

"Why are you so interested in this?" Abigail demanded. "Why does it matter to you?"

"It matters to me, because I'm trying to keep my sorry butt in the PVPD's good graces, that's why. Thanks to you and your family, I haven't had the best of luck with that, have I?"

"That was because of no wrong-doing on my part," Abigail snapped.

I held up my hands in mock surrender. "I know. Sorry, I shouldn't have brought that up. Taylor's an adult. Your daughter can make her own decisions. Anyway, do you remember your parents talking about it much?"

"Charlie's disappearance?" Abigail asked. "No. Why? Do you think my family had something to do with his death?"

"I didn't say anything of the sort," I insisted. "I'm just trying to find out what happened to him. Perhaps if I can give the police somewhere else to focus their attention, then maybe I can stay in their good graces for a while longer."

"Your insinuation wasn't appreciated," Abigail responded, tight-lipped.

"No insult intended," I insisted. "I just thought you might have been able to remember something pertinent. After all, you were, what, in your late twenties, early thirties when it happened?"

"I was only ten years old when that man disappeared," Abigail all but cried. Her face had turned red and she was clenching her fists with rage. "Do you really think a child could have pulled off a murder like that?"

"Ten?" I repeated, amazed. "Wow. Sorry. I'll be the first to admit that I suck at guessing people's ages."

"He really does," Jillian added.

"So, that means you're in your sixties," I mumbled, more to myself than anyone. "I wouldn't have called that."

Naturally, Abigail overheard.

"Is there a problem with that?" she snapped.

I shook my head. "Nope."

"Are your questions done?"

I looked at Jillian for confirmation. She emphatically nodded. Looking back at Abigail, I nodded once.

"We are. For the record, thank you for your cooperation."

"You can thank me by accepting my offer."

"I've yet to read it. As I mentioned before, it'll be highly unlikely that I'll agree."

"You assured me you'd consider it," Abigail insisted, growing angry once again.

"I most certainly did nothing of the sort," I responded, as my own anger grew. "I told you I'd read it, and only if you'd answer some of my questions. You answered them, for which I am grateful. Therefore, I will uphold my end of the bargain. I will read your proposal. But, as I previously mentioned, I am quite certain that I will be saying no."

Abigail stormed off, toward a few parked cars. Just then, Sherlock stuck his head through the Jeep's window and woofed. I could see that he was staring at Abigail. Shrugging, I snapped a few pictures.

On our way home, Jillian turned to me and nodded. "Well, I'd say that was proof positive that Abigail had nothing to do with Charlie Hanson's death."

"You don't know that," I countered. "Maybe she's sitting on the location of this lost gold mine, but hasn't acted on it yet."

Jillian shook her head. "Think about it. If a person like Abigail Lawson got her hands on an actual gold mine, then what would she need the winery for? She would have left you alone years ago."

I could only nod. She had a point. Abigail has always made it known that she craves money. If she had possession of Dawg's lost gold mine, then I wouldn't have to see her sorry face every six months or so.

FIVE

T wo uneventful days passed. And by uneventful, I mean wonderful. Glorious. In-
spiring. Why? Because it finally seemed like things
were calming down. Thanks to my cooperation
with the PD, I managed to slip off their radar. I
mean, I haven't been reinstated as a police consultant yet. But, it did seem like people have
finally realized there simply wasn't any way I
could be involved with the disappearance and/or
murder of Charlie Hanson.

Vance informed me that, since there were no
solid leads to pursue, the Charles Hanson case
would remain unsolved, and the file would be
placed back in their records room. What did that
mean for me? Well, with nothing to do with my
time, I decided to get started on the anniversary
surprise for Tori, Vance's wife.

For those of you who may not remember, I
agreed to help my buddy, Vance, with his fifteenth
anniversary present to his wife, Tori. How? Well, I

was asked to fashion a story with Tori as the protagonist. Now, that might sound difficult to pull off, but an idea had presented itself almost immediately after Vance suggested it, and since I had some time on my hands, I was eager to get going.

Since Tori had Irish roots, and she loved anything to do with the Emerald Isle, I was going to create a story based in County Cork, and set during the Great Potato Famine of the mid-19th century. Tori's character, who will be playing a widow, has to face unsurmountable odds as she struggles to keep her family alive and fed. With no family to turn to for help, will Tori's character be able to save her children when the people of her village, of her country, were dying of starvation?

Vance assured me Tori would love it, and since their anniversary wasn't until March of next year, I had some time to fine-tune the story, flesh out the characters, and jot down the beats for each chapter. And, that was exactly what I was doing. Well, it was what *we* were doing.

I was presently sitting in one of my house's spare bedrooms, which I had turned into my writing studio. The corgis were allowing me to write, and by that I mean they were out cold. Both were asleep on the small loveseat I kept in the room, specifically for this purpose, if you must know. Joining the dogs on the couch was Jillian, who was sitting quietly, legs crossed, and gently stroking Watson's fur with her right hand. She had her phone open and was poking around online while I scribbled away in one of my many notebooks.

Once I had finally completed my thought, and had successfully transferred it to paper, I expectantly looked up. However, I saw that both my dogs were asleep, and Jillian was playing some type of game on her phone. Confused, I glanced down at my notebook and was surprised to see I had filled nearly six pages with notes.

"How long has it been?" I asked.

She looked up while sliding her phone back into her purse. I also noticed Sherlock cracked an eye open to regard me for a few moments. Satisfied I wasn't leaving the room, the tri-colored corgi promptly went back to sleep.

Jillian checked her watch. "About twenty minutes."

"Really? Wow. I had no idea I had been writing that long. I'm sorry."

Jillian waved off my concerns. "No, don't worry about it. From the look in your eyes just now, I could only assume you had been whisked away someplace, and were desperate to get everything conveyed to paper."

"An apt description," I decided, as I gave her a smile. "I was back in Cork, Ireland, imagining what the city must've looked like 150 years ago. I was comparing what I was seeing in my head to what the town actually looks like, and was making a comparison of the differences." I tapped the notebook. "That's what I was doing. I need to try and create a believable setting."

Jillian rose to her feet, came around the desk, and placed a hand on my shoulder as she leaned down to look at my notes. After a few minutes, her eyebrows rose and a smile appeared on her face. Her hand started squeezing my shoulder, as though she was giving me a massage.

"Very descriptive. It's like you were really there. Wait. Have you? Been to Cork, Ireland?"

I nodded. "I have. A few years back, after setting one of my stories in Ireland, and then writing two sequels to it, I decided to view the Emerald Isle up close and in person. After I slipped up and revealed who my nom de plume was, I had the Lord Mayor of Cork asking me the same questions that you had just asked. Have I ever been there? How could I get so descriptive? Did I know the mental image I was painting would be so realistic that, for the eighteen months separating the books' releases, their tourism would jump by over two hundred percent?"

"The Lord Mayor?" Jillian repeated. "Did you make that up, or is that what the mayor is called?"

"He's the closest approximation to what we think of as the mayor," I answered. I looked up from my notebook and took Jillian's hands in my own. Unbeknownst to me, both dogs woke up for this and watched me through narrowed eyes, as though they didn't trust either of us to behave ourselves. "Lord Mayor is the title given to the Chairman of Cork City Council. He's essentially the local government body for the city, elected to office each year by the other members of the Council."

"How do you know so much about it?" Jillian wanted to know. "Oh, don't tell me. You wrote about it in one of your books."

I shook my head. "Nope. I looked it up online, just like I did several years ago."

Jillian laughed. She caught sight of a folding chair—currently folded—leaning against the wall near the closet. She pulled the chair over, unfolded it, and set it up directly next to me. That simple act earned a huge smile from me, but I did finally notice both dogs. Sherlock had fixed me with an intense stare, while Watson looked as though she was about to rouse herself to resume her duties as chaperone.

"Everything is cool, guys," I told the dogs. "There's no need to bark, or woof, or drool, or whatever else you two might be thinking of."

Surprised, Jillian turned to Sherlock and Watson and offered each of them a smile.

"Go back to sleep. We're just talking about your daddy's latest project."

Watson seemed satisfied with this, and closed her eyes. Sherlock watched the two of us for an additional ten minutes before he finally drifted back to sleep.

"Can I tell you again how sweet I think this is?"

I had been skimming through my notes when I looked up. I grinned, shrugged, and dropped my gaze back to my notebook. Just then, a soft hand dropped over mine. Looking up again, I immediately noticed Jillian was leaning close and gazing at me with an unreadable expression.

"What? Is something wrong? You don't like the premise of the story?"

Jillian shook her head. "I didn't say that at all. What I did say was this project, what you're doing for Vance and Tori? It's incredibly sweet of you."

I nodded. "Roger that. At least, I heard that part."

"Did you hear me say that I think I'm the luckiest girl in the world?"

I blinked at her a few times. Huh? I most certainly had not!

"Er, no. Really? Wow."

"I'm just teasing you, Zachary."

"You could have said anything just then, and I probably would have admitted it," I said, with a grin. I tapped my notebook. "Time has a tendency to slip away from me while I'm in here."

"Trust me, it's okay," Jillian assured me. "So, is this the part when I say I have another idea for you?"

I glanced down at my desk, at the pages of hastily written notes, and my eyes widened. That's how this whole ordeal had started. My lovely partner had said she had an idea for the book, and I went for a notebook. Now, nearly thirty minutes later, it looked as though history was going to repeat itself.

I looked over at Jillian, took a deep breath, and

began stretching my fingers. I flipped my notebook open to a new page, gripped my mechanical pencil tightly in my hand, and rotated my neck in a visible effort to remove any kinks. I took a few more deep breaths before I finally announced I was ready.

By this time, Jillian was laughing hysterically. Just then, the theme song from *Hill Street Blues* started playing. Grinning sheepishly, I reached for my cell.

"Who is it?" Jillian wanted to know.

"Vance. I finally switched out my old Twisted Sister ringtone for a friendlier one."

"It's appreciated by all," Jillian said, nodding.

"Hey, Vance, what's shaking? I think you should know, I have a working outline for … what? Excuse me? Hang on, pal, I'm putting you on speakerphone. What? No, only Jillian is with me." I set the phone on my desk and activated the hands-free option. "Now, would you say that again?"

"Hi, Jillian. Umm, okay, here it goes. There's been a murder."

Jillian covered her mouth in shock while my eyes widened with surprise. I heard collars shaking, so I glanced over at the couch to see both Sherlock and Watson on their feet, watching me intently. After a few moments, both corgis jumped down and joined us at the desk.

"Did I just hear Sherlock and Watson?"

"Yes."

"Good. We're going to need them."

"I thought my status of police consultant had been put on hold?"

"It was, now it isn't, by order of Chief Nelson. He wants you with me on this case."

"Wh-who was it?" Jillian quietly asked. "Do we know the identity of the person who was killed?"

"We do, but I'm not at liberty to say," Vance said, with a sigh. "We've yet to notify next of kin, let alone locate them."

"Perhaps I can help?" Jillian suggested. "I know everyone in town."

"I know you do, Jillian, only it won't help us this time. The person we're trying to reach lives in San Francisco."

"Oh."

"I'm putting leashes on the dogs right now," I told my friend. "Where do we need to go?"

"A Lazy Afternoon."

The bookstore? Alarmed, I looked over at Jillian. She, on the other hand, was staring at the phone, open-mouthed. Either the victim was Clara Hanson, or else someone had been murdered in her store!

"Tell me Clara is okay."

" I shouldn't have said that."

"Tell me she's okay," I insisted.

"Step on it, buddy. We could really use you here."

"Oh, no," Jillian breathed. She took my hand in hers. "You guys be careful, okay? Let me know what's going on as soon as you're able to, all right?"

I kissed her on the way out the door. "Will do."

It felt like the drive to town took three times as long as it should. I kept replaying the one question I had, which hadn't been answered, over and over in my head: was Clara the victim? Had someone murdered her in her own store? Granted, she could be annoying, but I certainly would like to think that alone wasn't worth killing over.

I ended up parking my Jeep nearly two blocks away from A Lazy Afternoon, seeing how there was now a severe shortage of parking spaces. Fire trucks, police cars, and an ambulance or two had taken every available space, including both sides of the street. Stepping up to the front door, I was in the process of pulling out my wallet to show my ID when the cop--assigned to keep out the public --noticed my dogs. Giving Sherlock and Watson a friendly pat, he lifted up the crime scene tape and waved us through.

Figures. My dogs get way more recognition than I ever will. Lately, a simple walk through the park would draw enough attention and admirers to make an outside observer think someone had to be throwing away handfuls of money. Whatever. I really didn't mind.

"Zack, over here."

I looked over a rack of books, in the direction where Clara's counter and cash register should be. The dogs and I had only made it a few steps before I heard a mad fluttering of wings. Just like that, Ruby had appeared on my shoulder, shaking uncontrollably. I remembered seeing Clara reach up with her hand to scratch Ruby on the top of her head. Anxious to see if the simple gesture would calm her down, I gave it a try. As luck would have it, the little parrot calmed considerably and nestled up against the side of my face.

"It's okay, Ruby," I soothed, as I gently ruffled the soft feathers on the top of her head. "Everything is going to be okay." At this point, I noticed Vance, standing on the other side of the counter, as though he was ready to wait on customers. "You don't have to say it. I already know. The victim was Clara, wasn't it?"

Vance solemnly nodded. He gestured at my shoulder. "Looks like you've picked up an admirer. I was beginning to wonder what we were gonna do with that bird."

I gazed at my friend, with confusion evident on my face.

"He likes you," Vance pointed out. "That means we should…"

"She," I corrected. "Ruby is an African gray parrot, and is a she."

"There's her cage, right over there," Vance said, as he pointed at the wrought iron black cage sitting behind the counter.

"Why are you telling me that?" I wanted to know. "Do you want her back in the cage for some reason?"

"No," Vance said, shaking his head. "I just thought you'd like to know where it was, so that it wouldn't take you too long to find it later."

"Why would I need to find it later?" I suspiciously asked.

"Because," Vance answered. He pointed at Ruby again. "Someone is gonna need to take care of her. Clara didn't have any family in town. From the looks of things, Ruby has already chosen another owner."

"Swell," I grumbled. I looked down at the dogs. "So, what would you like us to do? Check out the area? Umm, where was she found?"

Vance pointed straight down. "Right about here. She, er, had been worked over pretty good."

"Worked over?" I curiously repeated. "What's that supposed to mean? Are you saying someone beat her?"

Vance pulled out his notebook and flipped through the pages. "She had multiple abrasions, contusions, and lacerations. Zack, someone thought the vic had something they wanted, and they weren't gonna leave until they got it. The M.E. says she must have put up one heckuva fight. Say, when did you see her last?"

"A few days ago," I told my detective friend. "We broke the news to her that her father's remains had been found."

"How did she take it?" Vance wanted to know.

I shrugged. "How do you think she took it? She was sad. And angry."

Vance looked up. "Angry?"

"Right. She was only sad for a few minutes."

"What was she angry about, did she say?"

I nodded. "She wanted to know what her dad was doing all the way out in the middle of no-where. Clara mentioned her house—at the time—was located in the middle of town. She said some-one must have lured her father all the way out of town, because he didn't have any business being out there."

Vance nodded and continued to write in his notebook. After a few moments, Vance looked up and made eye contact with me. "You said she was also sad?"

"Wouldn't you be?" I countered. "She told us that she spent quite a few days putting up flyers, going door-to-door, and doing whatever she could to try and track down her father."

"Got it. Anything else I should know?"

I nodded. "She told us Charlie worked a num-ber of trades, presumably looking for a profession which paid more than the others. Get rich quick schemes come to mind. Clara said her dad was always trying something, and expected his ship would be coming in at any time."

Vance grunted once. "Makes me wonder if one of these schemes might've gone south?"

I shrugged. "It crossed my mind, too. I'm just wondering… well, that is to say, I wonder if…"

"…if the same person who killed Char-lie might've killed Clara?" Vance finished. "I've thought of that, too. Trust me, we're looking into it, only I have to say that I think it highly unlikely."

"Why?" I asked, confused. "If Charlie Hanson had something that was worth killing over, wouldn't it be possible for that same someone to think his daughter now has it?"

"Why now?" Vance asked. "And why here? This is a bookstore in the middle of downtown PV. If you want to cap someone, then there are certainly more discreet ways to do it."

"I still think they're related," I insisted. "It's too coincidental."

Vance turned to me and studied me for a few moments. "All right. Let's assume the two deaths were perpetrated by the same person and ignore the fact that our killer would have to be a senior citizen by now. Let's also assume the perp was looking for something that Charles had, but now believes the daughter has it. What could it be?"

I pointed at my friend's notebook. "Hey, you said it yourself: someone had worked poor Clara over. You don't do something like that unless you want something, and from the sounds of it, whatever they were looking for, my guess is they didn't find it."

"How can you be so certain?" Vance asked. He swept an arm around the store's interior. "If they didn't get what they were looking for, then don't you think they would have searched this place?"

"Unless they knew that, whatever it is, it wouldn't be found in a place like this," I argued. "Maybe it's something big? Maybe it's something that wouldn't fit in here?"

"Did Clara give any indication she knew what her father was killed over?" Vance wanted to know.

I shook my head. "No, but we did theorize it was something more than likely related to the Lost Cabin Gold Mine."

Vance blinked his eyes a few times at me as he let that last comment sink in.

"The Lost Cabin Gold Mine? Wait. Why have I heard about this? Wasn't this ... doesn't this have something to do with ... oh, what was that guy's name?"

"Red Dawg?" I prompted.

Vance snapped his fingers. "That's it. Thanks. You think Clara's father might have been killed over some childhood fable?"

"I know it sounds ridiculous," I began, "but..."

"...the lost gold mine," Vance interrupted. "I'll be darned."

"What?" I wanted to know. "What is it?"

"Red Dawg's lost mine is very well known here in town."

"Because it's supposed to be here somewhere?" I guessed.

Vance nodded. "That's right. Can you imagine what you'd do with a gold mine full of unmined gold? Wow. The possibilities are endless."

A cell phone chimed loudly, signifying the arrival of some type of message, be it e-mail or text. Vance eyed me, expectantly. I shook my head and pointed back at him.

"That wasn't me, pal. Mine sounds like a dang cricket."

Surprised, Vance pulled out his cell, tapped the display, and grunted once.

"I'll take that as a yes," I decided. "You deal with that. We're going to look around."

Vance nodded and began typing something on his screen. Giving the leashes a gentle shake, I nodded in the direction of the store.

"Come on, you two. We're here, so let's do our job, okay? Let's see if there's anything worth noting around here."

Sherlock rose to his feet, gave himself a good shake, and promptly moved off, with Watson hot on his heels. I followed the dogs into the heart of the store and slowly walked up and down each aisle. We had just stopped by an endcap displaying the works of a famous author and his latest release when both dogs stopped. Sherlock's ears were up, his nose was lifted, and I could hear him sniffing the air. After a few moments, both dogs situated themselves by the rack and turned to look up at me.

"What? You can't tell me this guy's books are better than mine. I've read a few. His are totally predictable. Mine aren't."

Darned if both dogs didn't snort, in perfect unison, as if to say they had a different opinion. I stepped up to the display and studied the books. Techno-thrillers, illustrated historical

novels, and a few bite-your-nails murder mysteries sat on the shelves, along with a few odds and
ends. Looking down at the dogs, who only had
eyes for the display, I sighed. Pulling out my cell, I
snapped a few pictures and, just like that, we were
moving on.

We ended up stopping three other times, all
in different locations throughout the store. Two
featured prominent authors and their newest releases, and the third had a display of knick-knacks,
created by some local artist. Before the dogs could
give me the stink-eye, I snapped photos of everything before us.

The dogs ignored everything else in the store.
That is, until we reached Clara's back storeroom,
which was nothing more than an enlarged utility
closet. Sherlock sniffed at the back door, which
I'm guessing led to the alley behind the store, and
promptly sat.

"We're not going out there, okay? In case you
didn't know, there's a small alley running between
the rows of stores. That's all there is. I'll be darned
if I let you lead me to some dumpster. The most
you'll get out of me will be a picture, okay?"

The dogs seemed satisfied with this, and once
the picture had been taken, led me back to the
counter, where I could see Vance pacing. He was
still on the phone; he looked up at me, and waved
me over.

"What's up?" I whispered.

Vance muted his call. "Did you guys find anything? Was there anything Sherlock … what's that? No, sir. We're investigating all possible leads. Yes, sir, I'm sorry to confirm Clara Hanson is dead and … yes, sir. The rumors are correct. It would appear someone worked her over. What they were trying to get her to disclose, no one can say. Yes, sir, as a matter of fact, they're here now. I don't know. I will let you know as soon as I do."

My friend sighed, slid his cell into a pocket, and faced me. "Did you know Chief Nelson's wife and Clara Hanson were close friends?"

"Oh, brother," I moaned. "Let me guess. The chief wants the person responsible for this found."

"Like, yesterday," Vance grumbled. He looked down at the two corgis, squatted, and produced two dog biscuits. "All right, you two. Did you find anything in here? Anything useful?"

"I led them around the store," I dutifully reported. "They stopped at several displays."

"Which ones?" Vance wanted to know.

I led the dogs back into the store and we retraced our steps. "These three with the books and that one over there, the one you can just make out."

"No books? The one with all the PV souvenirs on it? Keychains, candles, and shot glasses?"

I nodded. "That's the one. I don't know what it means, but I did take pictures of everything."

"Good. We'll have to study them later. Now, listen, Chief Nelson was telling me that they finally tracked down Clara's next of kin."

I nodded. "That's good, right? Who was it? Some niece or nephew?"

"Neither." He pulled out his notebook and flipped a few pages back. "One Darla Chantal Hanson. Get this. She's Clara's daughter."

"You learn something new every day," I decided. "I didn't know Clara had any kids."

"That makes two of us. Apparently, it's just the one, and they really didn't get along too well."

"I wonder why," I softly mused.

Vance shrugged. "Who can say? You know what Clara was like. Maybe her daughter disapproved of her behavior?"

"This is the one who was living in San Francisco?" I asked.

"Right. I'm told she'll be arriving tomorrow. From what I hear, she'll be taking over ownership of the bookstore."

SIX

The following day, the dogs and I were at Jillian's house, trying to learn as much as we could about Red Dawg's lost gold mine. Like her newly opened bed and breakfast, Highland House, Jillian's home was also listed among the historic houses which called Pomme Valley home. And, like all the others that could be found in this town, it had a name: Carnation Cottage.

To say the house was gorgeous would be an understatement. Then again, what would you expect? Jillian Cooper is a lady of high standards and exquisite tastes. I mean, her favorite champagne sells for $400 a bottle. So, it really didn't come as any surprise to me that I regarded her home as being the most beautiful house I had ever clapped eyes on.

Carnation Cottage was a large, two-story Victorian house which incorporated many of the characteristics one would expect to find in a period home such as this. Those included steep, multi-faceted roofs, decorative trim all across the house, textured wall surfaces, a one-story porch, and rounding off the list was the presence of a tower, complete with a steeply pointed roof.

The first thing most people noticed was that Carnation Cottage had a huge, wrap-around porch with a wrought-iron railing. Then, there was the manufactured stone siding, which consisted of a variety of gray colors. The rockwork stretched from the foundation of the house up to the roof line. Jillian explained that, while she wanted to use real stones on the house when she was having it renovated, the manufactured stone was simply the better choice. Not because of price, mind you, even though the manufactured stone was significantly cheaper, but it was due to the weight of the real stone. Unless she stripped the house down and reinforced the framing, the house wouldn't have been able to support the weight.

Manufactured siding it was, she had told me, with a smile.

I know what you're thinking. Once Jillian and I are married, I would end up moving in here. And trust me, I am strongly considering it. All you'd have to do is look at the old, country-style farmhouse I was currently living in and you'd be advising me to pack my bags and move. However, I was surprised to learn that I really enjoyed the open countryside of my winery. A visit to my nearest neighbors would require either a long walk or a quick trip in the car. Granted, my house wasn't out in the boonies, but it was fairly private.

I really wasn't too sure how it was going to work out. Neither Jillian nor I have given it too much thought. If only there were a way to swap the houses out, and put Jillian's Victorian house at the winery. Oh, well.

At the moment, the two of us were on the second story, in the southwestern corner of the house. This was Jillian's study, and man alive, did it make mine look inferior. Compared to this? My guest-room-turned-office looked like a kindergartener designed the room. I was seriously going to have to think about bringing in an interior designer.

Once again, I looked around the ornate study, noticing the fancy artwork on the walls, the glass sculptures on various display stands, and the big, executive desk against the far wall. Jillian turned to me to ask a question when she noticed I was slowly inspecting the room, as though I was taking inventory. She placed her hand over mine.

"What is it?"

"Hmm? Oh, it's nothing."

"Would you tell me?"

I shrugged. "Well, if you must know, I'm thinking I need to redo my own office. It pales in comparison to this."

"But I like your office," Jillian protested. "It suits you."

"Sure, it does," I agreed, and then sighed. "That's the problem. It's not very professional. I should really try to clean it up."

"Let me ask you something," Jillian said, as she returned her attention to the internet search engine she had open on her computer. She typed a new search query and, while the search populated the screen with results, turned back to me. "Has your office always been a spare room?"

"Yes. Why do you ask?"

"In that case, I think you shouldn't change anything. Why? Well, if you change your work environment, then—in all likelihood—you could end up changing the flow of your story. If you're happy with how things are, then you really should leave it be. Your office is your sanctum sanctorum. Don't change it."

"But..." I swept an arm around the professional-looking office we were both sitting in, "yours is so much cooler!"

"What works for me won't necessarily work for you," Jillian smoothly returned. "I don't spend nearly as much time in my office as you do in yours. That's ... oh, look! I think we might have found something."

I slid a chair over and eagerly sat down. "Whatcha got?"

"This, here. It's from Yreka. That's one of the locations Red Dawg is rumored to be linked to, isn't it?"

I nodded. "That's right. For whatever reason, Red Dawg traveled hundreds of miles each year, spending summers in Oregon and winters in

Northern California."

"Hundreds of miles?" Jillian repeated, as she frowned. "You do know where Yreka is, don't you?"

I nodded. "Sure, I guess. Northern California. It's near Sacramento, isn't it?"

Jillian opened a new window on the computer and quickly brought up a map of the state. In a few moments, a picture of the northern half of the state appeared on the screen. Using the zoom function on the map, Jillian zeroed in on the small area, right on the northern border of the state. I finally noticed what Jillian was trying to tell me as the picture continued to increase its size, displaying the names for the smaller-population towns. There, seemingly on the border of the two western states, sat Yreka. Surprised, I leaned forward to study the distance between PV and Yreka. There couldn't have been more than a hundred miles separating the two of us.

"Fifty-six miles, as the crow flies," Jillian reported. "I knew it was close, but didn't realize how close."

"Only fifty-six miles?" I repeated, amazed. "Okay, now I'm not as impressed."

"Not impressed? With what?"

"I thought our pal, Mr. Red Dawg, traveled hundreds of miles each year to gloat, or to visit family, or incur some other type of expense. He clearly had the means, why not show off a little? But, no. I don't think that's what he was doing. I think he did it only to throw people off his trail."

Jillian nodded. "To dissuade others into thinking his mine was there, in Yreka. Little did anyone know his mine was in another state altogether."

I tapped the computer's monitor. "Well, according to this account, people in California were growing suspicious of Dawg's wealth, and tried following him back to Oregon. It looks as though the townsfolk knew the mine wasn't local to them. Therefore, they tried to figure out the mine's location by stealth."

Jillian was silent as she skimmed the article. After a few moments, she inclined her head at the screen. "There. Do you see this?"

"What is it?" I asked, as I leaned close.

"One year, Mr. Red Dawg stopped coming. People started theorizing what had happened. The most common belief was that he had been ambushed and he had been killed."

"Theory two states it could have been an Indian attack," I read from the article.

"And the third theory is that he simply died out there, in the wilderness. As a result the Lost Cabin Gold Mine, as everyone seemed to be calling it, had truly become lost."

"I strongly doubt that it has remained undiscovered, to this day," I said, shaking my head. "Someone out there, somehow, has located the mine."

Jillian checked a few more sources before shaking her head. "It doesn't look that way, Zachary. If

Dawg's lost mine had been located, then someone would have reported it, don't you think?"

"I suppose."

At that moment, both dogs, who had been curled up on Jillian's thick, shag rug, rolled to their feet, gave themselves a solid shake, and then looked at the door. We may not have been at our house, but the meaning came through loud and clear: the dogs wanted to go outside. Anyone who has ever had to clean up an accident will back me up on this: whenever a dog indicates it wants to go outside, you will literally drop what you're currently doing and make sure the aforementioned animal makes it outside to do their business.

We rushed to the kitchen and I slid open the patio door. "After you, Your Royal Highnesses. Remember, there will be no doing your business on any of Jillian's flowers."

Surprisingly, both dogs ignored the freshly landscaped lawn, the weed-free gravel sections adjacent to the house, and—instead—headed east, away from the two of us.

"What the...? Where do they think they're going?" I demanded, as I stared at the retreating backsides of both my dogs. "Hey, you two! Get back here! Now's not the time to go sight-seeing, okay?"

I was ignored. Annoyed, I looked over at Jillian. "What lies in that direction?"

"Umm, there are a few fruit trees that way and my greenhouse."

"You finally had one installed? Good for you!"

Jillian smiled. "Thanks. It might be a tad small, but the size works for the area."

"Is there anything the dogs could get into, which would cause a problem?"

Jillian was silent as she considered. "Well, no, not really. I think it's okay."

I hurried out after the dogs. "It really isn't. They know not to go wandering off. Sherlock? Watson? Get back here, on the double!"

I'm going to have to consult with a dog trainer. The one command that neither of my dogs seemed to pay attention to was the 'come' command. No matter how hard I tried, or how foolish I felt (by getting all excited and energetic), neither dog would give me the time of day. Granted, they didn't ignore me every time I called, but it sure felt like it.

"I'll go get them. I'll be right back."

I stepped down off the veranda and followed the curve of the building as it turned east. There, directly ahead, was Jillian's tiny greenhouse. How tiny? Well, if you've ever seen the advertisements or floor plans on the internet for those Small Houses, I'd say it was that big. The walls were made of glass, the structure had a single gable, and the roof was covered with gray cement tiles. Turning to look back at Carnation Cottage, I had to smile. The small greenhouse looked like a miniature version of Jillian's home.

I found both corgis sitting before the door. As

I neared, Sherlock suddenly reared up on his hind legs, looked through the door's lowest window, and wiggled his nub of a tail in anticipation. He then looked at me, uttered one of his low howls, and promptly sat. Watson, content to do whatever Sherlock was doing, plunked her bottom down next to his.

Curious to see whether the greenhouse was locked, I tried the door. It swung open. Without waiting for my permission, both dogs hurried inside.

"What are you guys doing in here?" I demanded, as I ascended the steps. As I stepped inside, I was immediately assailed by the scents of wet earth, bags of topsoil, and some type of a chemical I could only assume was a liquid fertilizer. Running the length of the small greenhouse was a series of wooden racks, which had ample space for potted plants. Jillian, not one to waste the space, had every conceivable area filled with plants and flowers of some sort.

Sherlock and Watson, after taking a quick look around, angled straight for the back right corner of the tiny greenhouse. I could see row after row of young, green plants just starting to peek out over their pots. What they were, or were going to be, I hadn't the foggiest idea.

I started to pull the dogs away, but they wouldn't have any of it. Both of them slammed on the brakes and refused to be moved. Sherlock woofed once, reared up on his hind legs, and tried to get his nose up, over the edge of the top rack of plants. However, try as he might, the little corgi was just too short.

"What's with you? There's nothing up there but plants. Little ones. Fine. Here you go. I'm taking a picture. Will that satisfy Your High—?"

Just like that, the corgis lost their fascination with the racks of plants and immediately headed toward the door.

"I'll never understand dogs," I grumbled, as I closed the door behind me.

My cell started ringing. A quick glance at the display revealed it was an unknown number. Ordinarily, I'd just send it to voice mail, but I was also tired of people continually calling and not leaving messages. Whatever happened to common decency? If you call a person, and they're not available, then at least have the decency to tell the person why you're calling.

"Hello?"

"Mr. Anderson? This is Abigail Lawson."

Oh, crap on a cracker. Shoot me now. I knew I shouldn't have answered the phone.

"Ms. Lawson. Is there something I can do for you?"

"I just need to know if you're going to accept my proposal. Did you read it, like you promised?"

"I read it last night," I confirmed. "From start to finish."

"And?"

"And... I'm still not accepting. Whereas I'm appreciative of your honesty, telling me your plans to sell the winery to an outside corporation? Well, it doesn't change the simple fact that I want to keep the winery open in my late wife's memory. So, the answer to your very detailed proposal is still a resounding no. Now, will you let the matter drop?"

I was met with a stony silence.

"Abigail? Are you still there?"

"You're going to regret this."

The call was abruptly terminated. Sighing, I slid my phone into my pocket and glanced at the dogs. "Model citizen, huh?"

Back inside, the three of us headed upstairs. Jillian was waiting for us on the top step. "Is everything all right?"

"Yeah, they're both fine. They wanted to go into your greenhouse, presumably to look around. I took a few pictures."

"Sometime soon, something tells me we'll have to sit down and go through those pictures together."

"You're on," I said, as I grinned. "I also talked to Abigail Lawson. I gave her the official answer."

"How did she take it?"

"Not well, as expected. What else is new? So, have you found anything else out?"

Jillian nodded. "Possibly. Want to go on a road trip?"

"To where?" I asked.

"The library. As it turns out, according to their

website, they have a small section devoted to Red Dawg, and his importance to the Oregon State Gold Rush."

"You don't say?"

"I do say. Care to join me?"

"Absolutely."

"Will you leave the dogs here?"

"Here?" I scoffed. "Absolutely not. This isn't our house. I don't want to imagine what these two would do if they become bored."

"Zachary, you don't trust your own dogs?"

"If I'm in the room, then yes," I told her. "If I'm not, then not a chance. Your house is way nicer than mine. I'm not about to risk anything in here. Besides, the library is pet friendly. They can come with us."

Twenty minutes later, we strolled into the Pomme Valley Public Library. Jillian immediately angled toward the Information Desk, while I was stopped almost as soon as I had made it inside. Why? Well, blame the dogs' popularity.

"It's Sherlock and Watson!" a woman exclaimed. "Oh, look how cute they are!"

I looked at the owner of the voice. I really didn't have a clue who she was. Hopefully, I wasn't supposed to.

"I love these two dogs!" another voice exclaimed.

The owner of this voice was young, in her mid-twenties, I'd say. Her face was also unfamiliar.

"Are you guys working a case?" a male voice

asked.

I scanned the immediate area, but couldn't identify the owner. No one seemed to be looking my way.

I smiled politely, answered a few minor questions about the dogs, and then promptly excused myself. Jillian was beckoning me from the other side of the general seating area.

"I can't take you anywhere, can I?" Jillian teased.

I pointed down at the dogs, "Not with these two. What did you find out?"

"The lady at the counter said the Red Dawg section is somewhere over there, on the western wall. It's not that big, but it's all about *him*."

"That's rather convenient," I decided.

"It isn't," Jillian corrected. "According to the clerk, that particular display is set to be removed as soon as they get around to it. Now's our chance to see what they have."

"Roger that. Lead the way, m'lady."

Jillian slipped her arm through mine. "Thank you, kind sir. Sherlock, there's no need to woof. I'm not going to hurt your daddy."

I looked down at Sherlock just as the feisty corgi locked eyes with me. After a few moments, his gaze shifted to Jillian's and stayed there.

"It's okay," I assured Sherlock. "She's not going to hurt me. No woofing, please."

"They are very protective, aren't they?" Jillian said, as she leaned down and held a hand out to

Sherlock. "See? It's okay."

Sherlock hesitated for a few more moments before he finally gave Jillian's hand a lick.

"It's like having a four-legged chaperone," I sighed.

It took us a little longer than necessary to find the section dedicated to Red Dawg. I had expected to find either a dedicated shelf on a bookcase, or perhaps an entire case dedicated to all things mining and, perhaps, the region. In the end, we found what we were looking for only because Jillian stopped to tie her shoe.

"Oh, look! Zachary, this is it."

I turned to see Jillian tying her shoe, but she was crouched next to a glass display case. It was roughly four feet high, by about six feet long, and maybe four feet deep. Out for public display were a set of old mining tools, some period clothing, and a few other trinkets I was unable to identify.

"These are mining tools, huh?" I said, as I read the small display sign next to something I swear I've seen used as a murder weapon in horror films. "Look at that thing. What would a miner need with a two-foot-long metal spike?"

"It must be used for something," Jillian decided. "Well, it looks like that one is a lantern of some sort. And here's an assortment of picks."

"I thought this was dedicated to Red Dawg?" I quietly asked, as I walked around the other side of the display, as if a different perspective would reveal additional information.

In my case, it worked. There was an informational placard on my side of the case, and on it, it claimed that the items in the case belonged to Red Dawg himself. Skeptical, I glanced back at the items and frowned.

"There's a sign over here which claims all this stuff belonged to Red Dawg," I whispered to Jillian. "They couldn't know that for sure, could they?"

"In this case," a new voice announced, "they do."

We turned to see a young high school student standing behind us. From her nametag, I could see that she was one of the employees here at the library. I tapped the case with my finger.

"How much do you know about this?"

"Enough to answer questions," the brunette girl cheerfully replied. "What would you like to know about it?"

"How do you know these things once belonged to Red Dawg?" Jillian asked.

"Because we've had them in our library since before I was born," the girl answered. She then looked over at me as though she expected me to ask the next question.

"All right," I slowly began, "so, you've had these things a while now. Where did you get them from, do you know?"

The girl nodded, which caused her long tresses to tumble about. "The police department."

My eyes widened, and I returned my attention to the display case. These items were donated by the police? Could they be related to Charles Hanson's case? The police wouldn't willingly get rid of evidence, would they?

"Care to run that by me again? The police gave the library these things?"

"They didn't give them to the library," the girl clarified, "but, rather, they donated them. They said these items were from some case they were working, and since they didn't have the room to store them, and since they looked old, they asked if we'd be interested in displaying them in some fashion. We said yes, obviously."

"Oh, obviously," I agreed, earning myself a grin from the girl.

"What were the police doing with these things?" Jillian wanted to know.

"They were involved in some case," the girl answered. "That's all I know."

I squinted at the clerk's nametag. "Look, er, Pamela, is there any way you could confirm that for us? As well as the exact date you guys acquired them?"

"Can I ask why?" the clerk politely inquired.

"I'm a history buff. I only moved here a few years ago, and am always looking for anything that might have a piece of history attached to it. That's all."

"Everything is documented in the computer," Pamela informed me. "I'll go check. Stay right here. Oh, what cute dogs! I'll be right back."

Once the girl had left, I incredulously turned to

Jillian, and hooked a thumb at the display case.

"What are the chances this stuff might be related to the Hanson case?"

Jillian shrugged. "I'm willing to bet this *is* the Hanson case. No one could find out what happened to poor Charlie Hanson, and since they probably didn't know what else to do with this stuff, they got rid of it."

"I'm finding it hard to believe that the police would willingly give away evidence in an active investigation," I argued.

"Times change. Granted, I don't think the police would allow such a thing to happen in modern times, but obviously someone decided it was okay. Besides, it was no longer an active investigation."

"They said they were planning on removing these things," I recalled. "In that case, I say we ask whether or not they're being returned to storage, or else if the plan is to get rid of them."

Jillian nodded. "I see where you're going with this. Okay, she's coming back."

"You were correct," Pamela confirmed, as she nodded. "The notes in the computer say we obtained this collection of items in June of 1969."

"That's over a year after it happened," I softly murmured to myself.

Jillian cleared her throat. "Ahem, um, Pamela? One of the other clerks said that this display was earmarked for removal. Do you know what you plan on doing with these items?"

"Are you interested in acquiring them?" Pamela asked.

I nodded. "I most certainly would. My great-great-grand-uncle was a miner. Some of this stuff looks like it belongs in a mine. I'd hate to see such a fine collection thrown away or stored in some box in a dusty room for who knows how long."

"Would you like me to inquire about transferring ownership to you?"

I took Jillian's hand. "We would. Thank you, Pamela."

"Of course. I'll be right back."

I squatted down next to the dogs and threw an arm around each of them. Sherlock, familiar with this embrace, snuggled close and licked my arm. Watson, not to be outdone, burrowed her way past Sherlock to nestle in the crook of my elbow. I gave each of them a hug and a friendly scratching behind the ears. Several minutes of silence passed while we waited for Pamela to return. I continued to pet the dogs, while Jillian checked her phone for new emails. Upon hearing the telltale clicking of a pair of woman's heeled shoes approaching, I could see that our waiting was over. However, it wasn't Pamela who was approaching, but someone older. This lady looked to be in her seventies. A manager, perhaps?

"Good day to you. Would you be the couple inquiring about taking the collection of mining paraphernalia off our hands?"

I straightened, and after catching sight of the

amount of dog hair on my shirt, attempted to brush it off.

"That's us. I'm Zack Anderson, and this is Jillian Cooper. We were..."

My bad. I should've known what was going to happen. Sherlock, inexplicably, knew introductions were being made and, having been ignored, voiced his displeasure. One loud, exasperated bark of frustration echoed noisily around the quiet building. Every library patron, and I do mean *every* person currently in the building, looked our way. Shaking my head, I looked back at Pamela's manager.

"Are your ears bleeding yet? Mine sure are. Okay, sorry about that. If you'll look down, that's..."

"Sherlock and Watson!" the older woman happily exclaimed. "Oh my goodness! Look how sweet you two are!"

"You know my dogs," I chuckled. "I don't know why it surprises me anymore. Yes, these are them. Sherlock has the black on him. He's on your right. On your left is Watson. She's the red and white female."

The manager oohed and aahed over the dogs before finally straightening and, noticing she was now covered with dog hair, brushed at her clothes. Looking up at the two of us, she smiled.

"Jeanette Johnson. I'm the manager here at Pomme Valley Library. You are well known to us, Mr. Anderson. And you, Ms. Cooper. How could we forget our most generous benefactor?"

Benefactor? Turning to her, I was rewarded with a coy smile before Jillian took Jeanette's hand and gave it a firm shake.

"Hello again, Ms. Johnson. I'm sorry about Sherlock's bark. He doesn't like being left out of the introductions."

"Think nothing of it. Now, Pamela was telling me you'd like to take this collection of... things off our hands?"

I started laughing. "You were gonna say something other than *things*, weren't you?"

Jeanette plastered a smile on her face and started subtly nodding. "I have no idea what you're talking about, sir. Now, here's the thing. You'd like this collection? Congratulations, they're yours, only I can't give them to you. Yet."

"You need to find something else to put in its place," Jillian guessed.

Pamela nodded. "We already have something, but it's still being assembled. So, it might be a week or two, if that's okay. Plus, I've already notated it in the computer that the collection has a new owner."

"Perfectly fine," Jillian said. "Umm, do you know much about these things?"

Jeanette looked left, then right, and then dropped her voice so that only the two of us could hear it.

"This collection of junk, er, *things* was given to us because the police decided there wasn't anything else they could learn from it, so it was either find someplace to store it, toss it, or give it away."

"And this was from an active investigation?" I cautiously asked.

"It had been an active investigation," Jeanette recalled. "However, since the case was classified as unsolved, they felt it safe to donate the evidence."

"Are you referring to the Charlie Hanson case?" I wanted to know.

"As a matter of fact, I am. Are you familiar with the case?" Jeanette asked. "I wasn't working here when it was originally donated, but I do remember it was covered in the newspaper. Dark times, if you ask me."

"I can only imagine. From what I hear, it was the talk of the town."

Jeanette nodded. "Oh, it was. To think that one of PV's own had gone missing, well, it was unthinkable. This town had such low crime rates back then. That's why my family moved here."

I crossed my arms over my chest. "And now? Do you think it's really that bad?"

"In the last two years, PV has seen as many murders as Medford, even Bend! Do you think that's something we should be proud of?"

Vance's snarky comment about the increase of murders since my arrival in town suddenly echoed in my head. Maybe it *was* me. Perhaps I had brought some of the crime from Phoenix with me?

Dismissing the thought as ludicrous, I shook my head. No, it wasn't my fault. A sudden tapping focused my attention. Jeanette was now tapping thoughtfully on the glass display case.

"If you are really interested in learning more about PV's colorful history, especially when it comes to this particular case, then may I make a recommendation?"

"This particular case?" I carefully repeated.

Jeanette nodded. "Yes. This case. I've heard about the remains located on your property, Mr. Anderson. Is it true? Are they Charlie Hanson's?"

"Yes."

"Then, as I said, I would make a recommendation."

Jillian nodded. "And that is?"

"Find Derrick Halloway."

I pulled out my cell and did a quick search of the name.

"I've only heard the name in passing," Jillian admitted, "and I don't think I've ever met him. Who is he? A historian?"

"Mr. Halloway was the prime suspect in the Hanson case. They weren't able to pin anything on him, but everyone thought for certain he was guilty."

Interested, I leaned forward. "Oh? Do you know where we could find him?"

"I don't, I'm afraid. Last I heard, he was living on the outskirts of town, but that was a few years ago."

"Jeanette, you and Pamela have been fantastic. Here's my card. Would you give us a call when we can pick these things up?"

Jeanette was all smiles. "You're welcome, Mr. Anderson, and I will. Thank you."

"For what?" I asked, as I turned back around.

"For taking our ... junk ... off our hands."

Jillian and I both laughed as we headed outside.

"What now?" Jillian wanted to know.

"I have a pretty good idea where we can find Derrick Halloway," I returned, and then held up my phone. "I found a quick blurb about Derrick earlier this year. Apparently, he suffered some type of nasty fall and was taken to the hospital."

Jillian went sympathetic. "The poor soul. At their age, falls can be fatal. Did you find an address?"

"No, but I have a feeling I know where to find him."

"You do? Where?"

"At a nursing home. There's only one in town, so unless Mr. Halloway moved, which I don't think he did, and since the article mentioned he didn't have any family living nearby, then he should be there."

"Who would have put him in a nursing home?" Jillian curiously asked.

"The hospital. If there's no one to help care for an elderly patient once they're released from the hospital, then they'll typically go to a nursing home until they're well enough to care for themselves."

"How do you know this?"

"It's something my mother told me years ago."

"Ah. Very well. If we're going to a nursing home, then I'm really glad Sherlock and Watson are with us."

"You are? Why?"

"Dogs and nursing homes? They go hand in hand!"

Twenty minutes later, we were parking in the Visitor Parking of PV's one and only nursing home. I could see several residents sitting outside the visitor entrance enjoying the bright sunshine. As we approached, I couldn't help but notice two of the elderly residents' faces lit up with surprise and delight. The corgis, catching sight of the strangers, morphed into their Clydesdale personas and pulled me across the seating area until they had placed themselves directly in front of their wheelchairs.

"Who do we have here?" an old woman asked, as she reached a frail hand down to Sherlock's head.

"This is Sherlock," I began, as I gave him a scratch behind his ears, "and the other is Watson."

"Sherlock and Watson?" the old woman repeated, as a smile slowly spread across her face. "Like the detective stories?"

"Exactly like it," I confirmed. "As you can tell, they truly hate everyone they meet."

The old woman cackled with delight as she heaped attention on the tri-colored corgi. As for Watson, she had timidly approached the second wheelchair and was leaning her weight on the occupant's legs. The elderly man sitting in the chair stretched an arthritic hand down to rub her ears. I looked over at the second resident and saw he had locked eyes with me.

"Did I hear you say this little boy's name is Watson?"

I smiled at the senior and gave him a little nod. "Well, yes and no, actually. Yes, the name is Watson, but no, she's a female, not a male."

"This is a little girl dog?" the male resident hesitantly asked, as he looked up at me with a look of horror on his face. "What kind of name is that for such a cute little girl like her?"

Watson promptly flopped over, onto her back. The resident grinned, and then gave the little female corgi exactly what she wanted, a belly rub.

"Yeah, I'm thinking they're gonna have the times of their lives in here," I said, chuckling.

"Excuse me," Jillian said, as she drew each of the resident's attention. "Do either of you know a Mr. Derrick Halloway?"

The woman automatically shook her head, but the male resident slowly nodded.

"I think that's the name of the gentleman who is currently several doors down the hall from me."

"Has he been there long?" I asked.

The resident shook his head. "No, not long. Less than a year, I reckon."

We both thanked the resident, said our goodbyes, and stepped into the visitor center. Signs directed us to the counter, where we had to sign in. The friendly lady, upon seeing both corgis, assured us we were going to be the hit of the day and begged us to linger a little while to allow the rest of the residents a chance to meet the dogs. A sheet of paper was produced, which had a diagram of the complex on it, much like what you'd receive if you asked a hotel clerk how to find your room, and we were sent on our way. With directions in hand, and being properly signed in, Jillian slipped her arm through mine and, together, we headed down the hall.

We found Derrick Halloway's room without any problem, having only been stopped no fewer than five times. Bringing your dogs, who are already friendly to begin with, to a nursing home is a sure-fire way to make new friends. Everyone absolutely loved the corgis, and for the record, the corgis adored the attention. They, I'm certain, were having the time of their lives.

Seeing room #1015's door was open, I knocked loudly on the frame. After a few moments, when we didn't hear anything, I cleared my throat and tried again.

"Hello? Is anyone there? Mr. Halloway, are you awake?"

"Who's there?" a shrill voice demanded.

"My name is Zack Anderson. I'm here with my fiancée, Jillian, and two dogs. We'd like to come in and talk to you, if that's okay."

"Suit yourself," the voice harrumphed.

Glancing at Jillian and rolling my eyes, we stepped into the room. Immediately apparent was the pungent aroma of body odor. Based on the smell, Mr. Halloway hadn't taken a shower since … forever. My eyes had started watering and I threw a look at Jillian, which stated we wouldn't be staying long. Jillian nodded.

Lying on the bed, covered by a pale blue sheet, was Mr. Derrick Halloway. He looked to be in his late eighties, was thin as a rail, and wearing stained pajamas. He also had a week (or two) of scraggly growth on his face. His white hair was disheveled, he had candy wrappers and bags of empty chips scattered across his bed, and he had the TV on, set to some soap opera.

The occupant of the room finally shifted his attention off the television to give me a very brief once-over. Grunting once, he reached for the remote and unmuted the TV. Thankfully, the audio wasn't that loud. But, I also noticed his thumb was inching toward the volume up button on the remote.

"I'm sorry to bother you, Mr. Halloway. I was hoping we could ask you a few questions?"

"About what?" Derrick suspiciously asked.

"About what you can remember about the Charles Hanson case," I gently answered.

Now I had Derrick's full attention. His hand scrambled for the remote and he hastily muted the TV. He squinted his eyes as he stared up at me.

"Are you a reporter?"

"No. I'm just someone who wants to know what happened."

"I didn't kill him," Derrick whispered. "I don't know how many times I have to say it. Charlie was my best friend. I could never have hurt him."

Surprised, I looked over at Jillian. She nodded once, and then inclined her head, encouraging me to continue.

"Do you remember what happened?" I softly asked.

"Like it was yesterday," Derrick admitted.

"Would you tell us?" Jillian asked.

Derrick gazed at the two of us for a few moments before he finally nodded. "I don't know what your interest is in something that happened so long ago, but so far you haven't accused me of anything, so yeah, I'll tell you what I know."

"We appreciate it," I told Derrick. Right about then, I remembered passing a couple of folding chairs out in the hallway. I held up my hands in a time-out gesture and hurried out of the room.

"What's he doing?" Derrick asked, confused.

Before Jillian could answer, I re-entered the room, holding the two chairs. I set one for Jillian and then one for myself. Much to my surprise, I noticed that I had set them up as close as possible to Derrick's bedside.

Properly seated, I was about to encourage Derrick to continue his narrative when the dogs surprised me by jumping up onto Derrick's bed.

"Get down from there," I scolded. "I'm pretty

sure dogs aren't allowed up on the bed."

Derrick batted my hand away as I reached for Sherlock's collar. "Don't worry about it. They're fine. Hmm, wait a moment." He then extricated one of his thin arms from beneath his sheet and swept it across the top of his bed. Crumbs, wrappers, and bits of trash were flung to the floor.

Cringing, I automatically scanned the room, searching for a trash can.

"Leave it," Derrick said, correctly guessing what I was thinking. "The nurses just love it when I make a mess in here. Based on what I've done before, this is nothing but child's play." With the two corgis curled up on either side of him, Derrick sighed and began to speak. "Charlie Hanson was my best friend from childhood. We went to school together, we hung out together, and yes, we got into trouble together. What can I say? He had a way of getting me to do things I never would have dreamed of doing on my own."

"I have a friend like that," I said, chuckling.

"Hush," Jillian scolded.

"Sorry."

Derrick smiled at me and began petting Sherlock's back.

"He was energetic, enthusiastic, and full of piss and vinegar. He was so full of life that it was ... was..."

"...contagious," Jillian added, drawing a smile from the old man.

"Exactly, my dear. Now, if you knew Charlie,

you'd also know that he didn't always make the smartest decisions."

"We've heard about his 'get rich quick' schemes," I said, adding the necessary air quotes. "Were his decisions as bad as everyone seemed to think?"

"Worse. I was certain one of those hair-brained schemes was going to backfire on him."

"Maybe one of them did?" I suggested.

"You're referring to that mine, aren't you?" Derrick grumbled. "I told Charlie over and over it was just a myth. Would he listen? No. He was so certain he was on to something big that he wouldn't listen to reason."

"Do you think he found the mine?" I skeptically asked.

Derrick shook his head. "No. As I said, Red Dawg's mine was nothing but a myth."

"It's supposed to exist," Jillian quietly reminded him.

"Well, maybe it does, but it certainly isn't going to be found in PV," Derrick argued. "Charlie searched for years."

"Was that what he was working on when he disappeared?" I asked.

Derrick sighed and nodded. "Yes. The funny thing was, he made it sound like he'd made more progress than anyone else. I was actually starting to believe he had found something."

"He never told you what," Jillian guessed.

"That's right. If he made a breakthrough, then

it died with him."

"And you have no idea what he found?" I asked.

"If I did, then I sure wouldn't be in here, would I?" Derrick scoffed. "If I found that mine, then I'd have a bevy of private nurses at my beck and call. Why, I'd even build my own private hospital."

Sensing we weren't going to get any more helpful information out of Mr. Halloway, I caught Jillian's eyes and inclined my head at the door. As I stood up, earning me twin looks of derision from the dogs, Derrick looked over at me and shook his head.

"I never did figure out what he meant."

I hesitated. Meant? About what?

"About…?" I asked, trailing off in an attempt to get the elderly senior to complete the sentence.

"He said he had the key."

I blinked a couple of times and shared a quick look with Jillian. "Key? To what? Locating the mine?"

Derrick helplessly held out his hands. "I don't know. Those were the last words he ever spoke to me. Save yourself a lot of trouble and listen to me when I say … there is no key. I should know. I spent over ten years looking. I never found anything that could be loosely called a key."

"Perhaps it's not a physical key?" Jillian suggested.

Derrick nodded. "I thought of that, too. The only theory I could come up with was that he finally did it."

"Did what?" I wanted to know.

"I think Charlie did what he said he was going to do, and that was the key: he identified Red Dawg."

SEVEN

T hat certainly happened a lot faster than I thought," I said, a few days later. I glanced in the rearview mirror to make sure both corgis were behaving themselves. Granted, I wasn't too concerned about their actions in my Jeep, as opposed to Jillian's much nicer SUV, but I still wanted them to behave. As luck would have it, both were plastered to the windows, watching the passing scenery. "Think we'll find whatever Charlie found in that stuff?"

Jillian shrugged. "Are you referring to the key? Who can say? But, isn't it exciting to try? I mean, you never know what we'll find. Maybe there's something tucked away, locked inside something else?"

"Maybe they didn't display everything they were given," I added.

Jillian nodded. "A very distinct possibility." A few moments of silence passed. "I still think that message Jeanette left for you was adorable."

"In what way?" I wanted to know, as we passed Gary's Grocery on our way to the library.

"Don't you remember what Jeanette said? 'Come and get your crap, Mr. Anderson. Our next display is ready.' I can't believe she managed to say that with a straight face."

"Right?" I chuckled. "I wonder what prompted the rush? I mean, she told us that it wouldn't be ready to go for another week or two."

"Maybe they were looking for an excuse to get the next display set up?" Jillian suggested. "At any rate, who are we to argue? We wanted to learn more about Red Dawg, and seeing how that collection of items came from the police department after investigating Charlie Hanson's disappearance, now's our chance. Hopefully, there are a few secrets in there that are just waiting to be discovered."

I held up my right hand with a pair of fingers crossed.

"Here's hoping."

"Where are we going to store it?"

"Store what, the stuff from the library? I can always put it in a closet somewhere."

"And if it's more than one box?" Jillian countered.

I shrugged. "Well, there's a ton of room in the basement. I can always store it down there until we have a chance to go through it."

Satisfied with that answer, Jillian fell silent. Ten minutes later, while she waited inside the

Jeep with the dogs, I walked into the library to claim the contents of the Red Dawg exhibition. In this case, Jillian was right. There wasn't one, nor two, but three boxes of junk. Er, stuff. Eyeing the boxes in the back of my Jeep, I couldn't help but pop the lid off the closest one and take a look inside. What I saw had me grinning.

"What is it?" Jillian asked, as she appeared beside me. "See anything good?"

"Let's see. This box has what appears to be an oil lantern, at least half a dozen chisels, a spike thing with some type of hook for a hilt, and in this bag? I don't know. Looks like pieces of flint."

"And that box? What's in there?"

I gently lifted the lid to the shoebox-sized wooden crate and picked up a thick, semi-sorta slimy candle. I should also add that both dogs immediately perked up.

"Eww. This thing is disgusting."

"What is it?" Jillian wanted to know. She leaned forward and wrinkled her nose. "Tallow. I'm willing to bet this is a candle made out of tallow."

"Tallow," I repeated, as I brought up the definition, from memory. "A hard, fatty substance made from various forms of animal fat." My hand instantly sprang open and I dropped the nasty-old candle back into its box. "All right, I think I'm gonna be sick now."

"What's with them?" Jillian wanted to know.

I looked up and grinned as I saw my two dogs

peering at me from over the backseat. I quickly removed the two screws holding the Jeep's passenger side taillight in place and gently pulled it out of its holder. Visible behind the light was a small compartment. In it, I kept a roll of paper towels and a few wet wipes.

Baffled, Jillian leaned around me to stare at the opening, while I cleaned my hands as best as I could.

"Wh …what is this? Do all Jeeps have secret compartments behind their taillights?"

"This one does," I informed her. I placed the items back into the cubbyhole and reattached the taillight assembly. "A friend of mine in Phoenix also had a Jeep, but it was a few years older. He's the one who told me about these little storage compartments. So, ever since I got the dogs, I've kept some emergency cleaning supplies in there."

Jillian beamed a smile at me. "That's clever."

Twin woofs, which sounded an awful lot like corgi warning woofs, caught my attention. I looked back at the dogs, but they were seemingly looking at something behind me. Intent on seeing what it was, I turned, only to stifle a curse.

Two PV police cruisers had just pulled up in front of the Jeep.

"Mr. Zachary Anderson?" one of them sternly inquired.

"That's me," I said. I squinted as I stared at the policeman. "Wait a minute. I know you, and I know you know me. Officer Jones, isn't it? Would you care to tell me what this is about?"

Officer Jones looked at his partner and began reaching around his back. Curious, I watched as the policeman fumbled with something for a few moments before swinging his arm back around. My eyes widened as I saw the glint of metal. He was holding handcuffs! Did he intend to put those on me?

"What the hell is going on?" I demanded, growing angry.

"Zachary Anderson," the second cop began, "you're under arrest for the murder of Clara Hanson."

My eyebrows shot up. "Excuse me? Tell me you're not serious."

"You have the right to remain silent."

"I know I do. Would you two knock it off and just talk to me?"

"Anything you say can and will be used against you in a court of law," Officer Jones intoned.

Bemused and annoyed, I simply held out my hands and let the officer snap his cuffs on me.

"Zachary," Jillian protested, "aren't you going to say anything?"

"I'll wait for him to finish," I said, looking over at the second cop, which—for the record—I didn't recognize. "This has to be a mistake. I didn't kill Clara."

"He seems to think you did," Jillian argued.

"...will be provided for you. Do you understand the rights I have just read to you?" the second officer continued.

That's when I saw he had a tiny, plastic-encased white square in his palm. I couldn't help it. I started smiling.

"This is funny to you?" Officer Jones snapped.

I nodded at the second cop. "He doesn't know the Miranda Rights, and he's reading it from a teeny, tiny cheat sheet in his hand."

Officer Jones blinked a few times before turning to his partner, who had whipped his hand behind his back.

"Let me see what's in your hand."

The second officer shook his head. "No, it's nothing. Forget about it."

"Officer Martin, let's have it."

"You don't need to see it," Officer Martin curtly announced. "You already know it."

"What has the chief said about not knowing basic Miranda Rights?"

Officer Martin sighed. "He doesn't tolerate it. Fine. Here. Take it."

The laminated cheat sheet, no bigger than a business card, was thrust into Officer Jones' hands. He took one look at it and shook his head. Realizing others were present, a sheepish look appeared on both officers' faces.

"If you're arresting Zachary for the murder of Clara Hanson," Jillian hotly began, "then I assume you have some proof?"

Both officers nodded. "We do."

"And that is?" Jillian said, growing angry.

"We have uncovered a nasty voice mail, left by Mr. Anderson, on the deceased's personal cell phone."

"I don't even have Clara's personal cell phone," I sputtered. "You can check my cell. In fact, I insist you check my cell. You'll see that I haven't placed any calls to her. I haven't even called her store in over a year and a half!"

"When was this call supposedly made?" Jillian wanted to know.

"It was left the day of the murder," Officer Martin smugly added, as if that alone cemented my guilt.

"Voice mails can be faked," Jillian informed the officers.

"And a cell phone's call history can be deleted," Officer Martin curtly returned.

Jillian crossed her arms over her chest. I've seen her do that before. It meant she was seriously aggravated, and I'm thankful to say, it wasn't directed at me.

"I assume you have something more incriminating than a faulty cell phone report?"

Officer Jones sighed, looked at me, offered me an apologetic look. "We do. We have the murder weapon. It's covered in the victim's blood and has Mr. Anderson's fingerprints all over it."

Surprised, Jillian turned to me and held up her hands, in a what now gesture.

"I have no idea," I told her. "I think they're grasping at straws."

"What is the murder weapon?" Jillian wanted to know.

"It's a tire iron," Officer Jones announced.

That caught me off guard. A tire iron? With Clara's blood and my prints on it? How in the world could that be?

"A tire iron," I slowly repeated. I let my hands drop. "I don't even know what to say to that. I don't even own a tire iron. My Jeep has one of those little jacks, where the handle doubles as the lug wrench."

Offering me a sympathetic look, Officer Jones pointed at my Jeep. "When was the last time you changed a tire, Mr. Anderson?"

"In that thing? I haven't had to change a tire since I lived in Arizona. Feel free to check. I had my tires rotated during my last oil change, and one of the techs forgot to put everything away. I saw the jack then, if that helps."

"Could it have been mine?" Jillian asked. She looked over at me and shook her head. "You did change out one of my tires, but you used my tire iron and jack to do it."

I nodded. "True."

"When was this?" Officer Jones asked. A notebook had appeared in his hand and he started making notes.

I looked at Jillian. "Last year? Early this year?"

"November," Jillian reported. "November of last year."

Officer Jones checked his clipboard and was silent as he skimmed through the arrest warrant. "No, it says here that the only prints found on the four-way cross wrench was Mr. Anderson's. There were none others present."

"Whoa, wait a minute. Did you say four-way cross wrench?"

"What is that?" Jillian wanted to know.

"Ever see one of those tire irons that look like a big plus sign?"

"Yes, but only in auto-parts stores. Is that what you have? One of these special tire irons?"

I nodded. "I did, but not anymore. I had one in Phoenix, but I lost track of it. I always assumed it had been stolen."

Jillian paused as she considered the ramifications. "Taylor? Do you think Taylor could have stolen it while she was in Phoenix, stalking you?"

Taylor Rossen was the former beat reporter from the local newspaper. She also just so happened to be Abigail Lawson's daughter. When I first moved to PV, I had the misfortune of being accused of murder, and one of the pieces of evidence had my prints on it. Taylor later revealed that she had traveled to Phoenix, in an attempt to 'get to know' the person who had cheated her out of her inheritance and steal my prints (without me knowing about it). I wouldn't put it past her to have stolen a few things out of my Jeep while she was there.

However, while easy to blame Taylor, Abigail's daughter has been incarcerated for several years now, and has another twenty-plus years to go before she'll get to walk free. Therefore, it couldn't be her. Who else, then?

"Are you going to come willingly, or are you planning on resisting?"

That statement alone had me whipping my head around to stare at Officer Jones. It was clear someone was setting me up. Again. This time, though, I had quite a few friends in PV. I sincerely doubted the PVPD would be able to make any of the charges stick.

"No, I'll go willingly. This has been one mother of a mix-up. I'm no murderer. The sooner I can prove that, the better."

"I'll get you some help," Jillian promised, as I was stuffed into the back of a police cruiser.

The ride to the police station took nearly three times as long as it should. I could only assume Officer Jones had been ordered to parade me through the city, in an attempt to show the people that they had a suspect in custody. How I managed to end up in this situation—again—floored me. I thought these guys were my friends. I thought we had finally moved beyond the past charge of murder, which had been officially expunged from my record, thank you very much.

Walking through the station, I'm pleased to say that practically everyone we passed either had a look of incredulity on their face, or one of sheer curiosity. It would seem that not everyone had been privy to the chief's decision to formally charge me with Clara's murder.

Leaning back in the torn chair in Interview Room #2, which, of course, is the same room I was in before, I looked up at the clock on the wall. Fifteen minutes past three in the afternoon. I had soooo many other things I'd rather be doing right now. The door opened, and in came Chief Nelson, along with a stern, older lady I didn't recognize.

The chief nodded. "Mr. Anderson."

"Chief."

"This is Detective Myrna Stettle, from the Medford police department. She'll be handling this investigation. As you can imagine, Detective Samuelson has been removed from the case."

I nodded. "Understood. I'm told I'm here because you think I killed Clara Hanson? Are you serious?"

Chief Nelson shrugged. "While hard to believe, the evidence is rather damning, Mr. Anderson."

"You have a tire iron and a voice mail," I recalled. "Can I hear this voice mail? Seeing how I've never left one for Clara, I'd like to hear what it says."

Chief Nelson nodded, and calmly placed a small, black device on the counter before us. He tapped a single button on the surface and leaned back in his chair.

Now, I should point out that the voice did sound like me but, then again, it wasn't *quite* me. I don't know. There was something about it which made me think the voice was synthesized, if that was even possible.

Clara, I've absolutely had it with you. You're a disgrace to everyone in Pomme Valley, and you deserve everything that's headed your way. Enjoy it while it lasts.

Chief Nelson looked back at me and cocked his head, as if to say, Well?

"I'll tell you right now that I never left that. And ... doesn't it sound a little mechanical?"

The chief leaned forward. "What do you mean?"

"Well, listen to it. The tone of the message never changes. It's like we're listening to a robot speak."

"A robot," the female detective scoffed. "Is that the best you can do, Mr. Anderson?"

I ignored her and kept my attention on the chief. "Check my phone records. You'll see that I didn't send that at all."

"We've already accessed your cell phone records," the chief pointed out. "We could ping the cell tower closest to your winery. The call originated from there. It had your caller ID attached to it."

"Couldn't someone have played that message on speakerphone, from another cell?" I asked, frowning.

"You're grasping at straws," Detective Stettle smirked.

"All I'm saying," I pressed, as I continued to

146

ignore Detective Needstofindaman, "is that those calls can be faked."

"How do you explain this?" Detective Stettle snapped.

I slowly turned to face the female detective and, don't ask me why I did this, but I deliberately cocked my head, as if I just now noticed she was there. Hey, two can play this let's-be-a-jerk game.

"How do I explain what?" I innocently asked.

Detective Stettle reached under the counter and plopped something in a large, sealable plastic bag on the counter. It clanged loudly in the small room. Glancing down at the item, I could instantly see that it was a four-way cross wrench, the same one Officer Jones had described to me in the library parking lot. And, darned if it didn't look just like the one I had, back in Arizona.

I sighed. It obviously was the one I had in Arizona. How, then, did it end up here?

"I can tell from your expression that you recognize it," Detective Stettle smugly informed me. "Now, we're getting somewhere."

"I haven't seen that thing since before I lived in Pomme Valley," I said, as I shrugged. "During the winter months in Phoenix, the weather is gorgeous."

"How is this pertinent, Mr. Anderson?" Detective Stettle asked, with exasperation evident in her tone.

"Because," I slowly explained, "in Phoenix, during winter, average temps are around sixty to seventy degrees. You should have something in front of you which states I own a 2014 Jeep Wrangler Rubicon. Granite crystal color, if you must know. My jeep has a hard top, which I would remove when the weather was nice. What was the result? Well, it essentially meant I couldn't leave anything of value inside my car, because anyone would be able to reach inside from the outside. Am I going too fast for you?"

Detective Stettle scowled and crossed her arms over her chest

"Now, during the winter months, it's so nice in Phoenix that I, and most other Jeep owners, would take the hard tops off to enjoy the sun and the fresh air. Are you still with me?"

The lady detective didn't say a word. The chief, on the other hand, had the beginning of a smile on his face.

"Anyone could have taken that tire iron. Honestly? I thought I had misplaced it and lost it during the move from there to here."

"Are you finished, Mr. Anderson?" Detective Stettle all but snarled.

"Nope." I pointed at the stack of paperwork opposite me on the countertop. "I'm sure that, somewhere buried in that pile, is the report of the first time I was charged with murder. Who ended up being responsible? A lady by the name of Taylor Rossen. She's the one who traveled to Phoenix from here, mind you, to stalk me and obtain my prints."

"Are you suggesting Ms. Rossen, who is currently incarcerated, by the way, is responsible for framing you?" Detective Stettle snidely asked.

"Wow. Remind me to never move to Medford."

Chief Nelson snorted, but quickly disguised it as a series of coughs.

"I can't say if Taylor is responsible," I explained. "I'm just giving you an example of what could have happened."

"And how do you explain all the past references to Ms. Hanson?" Detective Stettle asked. She pointedly selected one of the folders on the table and opened it. Deliberately skimming each line with her fingertip, she stopped about halfway down the page and started tapping it. "'Clara Hanson is a pain, and she creeps me the hell out.' That's a direct quote, Mr. Anderson."

Where on earth did she get that? What, am I being bugged now? I deliberately kept my mouth shut as I struggled to decide how to make a rebuttal to that.

"You're right. That does sound like something I would say. I can only..."

"'Someone needs to put her in her place'," Detective Stettle continued, interrupting me. "'She doesn't respect a person's privacy, and that's gotta stop'. Ring any bells?"

I just stared at the lady detective, with my mouth open, I'm sure. I may not have remembered saying all those things, but that one particular line, about putting Clara in her place, was one

I remembered quite well. I should, seeing how I only said it last week, while at lunch with Vance and Harry. And nowhere, might I add, was there a microphone or tape recorder that I could see.

"You surprise me, Detective," I said. "Bugging a private conversation, without permission?"

"I did no such thing," Detective Stettle all but sputtered.

"Recording in-person conversations, in the great state of Oregon, is only allowed if both parties consent," I intoned, as if I was reciting from a book. "Guess what? I didn't consent. Besides, that snippet was taken completely out of context."

"This was provided by a reliable source," Detective Stettle sourly responded.

I looked at Chief Nelson and gave him a what-can-you-do shake of my head. The head of the Pomme Valley police actually appeared apologetic, but unfortunately, didn't volunteer anything else. At that exact moment, the chief and the detective locked eyes, and darned if I didn't see a look of disgust pass from the one to the other. Care to venture a guess as to the identity of the person who was disgusted?

"Never once," I said, as I focused all my attention on the visiting detective, "have I ever threatened Clara in any way, shape, or form. To suggest I have is ... and I'm going on record here, so feel free to take as many notes as you like. To suggest I have is an insult. Further, seeing as how I have never consented to have any of my private conversations recorded, since I am allowed to have my own private thoughts, you will refrain from ever repeating them again. Have I made myself clear, Detective Stettle?"

"You forget yourself, Mr. Anderson," the detective angrily returned. "You're the one sitting on that side of the table, with a murder charge over your head."

The door immediately opened and a woman slightly younger than me, wearing a pressed, navy blue skirt suit, stepped into the room. She walked around the table, motioned for me to stand up, then faced Detective Stettle.

"Good afternoon," the woman announced, although body language and tone of voice suggested she had no desire to wish the chief or the detective any such thing. "My name is Deidra Akins. I will be representing Mr. Zachary Anderson from here on out. Now, I've reviewed the charges against my client. I am honestly surprised that you would bring charges against one of your own."

"One of our own?" Detective Stettle scoffed. "Please. He's just a consultant who..."

"...who has solved more cases than you, Detective Stettle," my lawyer smoothly returned. "Let's review. Aside from this one, you've handled three murder cases in the last five years. One was categorized as unsolved, and the other two took, on average, seven months for an arrest. Now, my client alone has handled three times that many cases, has solved all of them, and each of them took no longer than a few weeks."

Detective Stettle muttered something, but I couldn't make it out.

"I'm sorry, Detective," Deidra said, looking up from her pile of paperwork. "Did you say something?"

"No."

"I didn't think so. And that concludes our business. Mr. Anderson, come with me. Your bail has been posted. You are a free man."

"This isn't over, Mr. Anderson," Detective Stettle vowed. "Don't plan on leaving town."

"You're right," Deidra said, as the two of us stepped outside, into the corridor. "It's not. I'll expect a full apology in less than forty-eight hours."

"When hell freezes over," came the detective's reply, just before the door slammed shut.

"Okay, who are you?" I asked, as I fell into step behind Deidra. "Did Jillian send you?"

"Jillian is a dear friend of mine," Deidra confirmed, as she led me through an open doorway.

"Are you based here, in PV?"

"Medford," Deidra answered.

"Medford," I scoffed. "Tell me something. Do you have a history with Detective Stettle back there?"

Deidra turned just then, and flashed me a smile. "We do, indeed. As soon as I saw her name on the arrest warrant, I volunteered to take the case, pro bono."

"Well, I appreciate it. If there's anything I can

do for you, then please let me know."

"There is one thing, Zachary."

"What's that?"

"Having heard so much about them, I'd like to meet your dogs. Corgis have to be one of my favorite breeds. What do you say?"

"Deal," I said, as I thrust out my hand.

"Wonderful. Consider me on your case."

EIGHT

W hat did I do to deserve this?" I lamented, the following day. "I mean, I try to be nice to people, treat them with respect, and this is the thanks I get?"

"I'm still upset that the PVPD leveled charges at you," Jillian quietly told me. "After all you've done for them? I hope you consider telling them you won't be returning as a consultant after all of this is said and done."

"Oh, I'm seriously considering it," I admitted. "Let's see how well they do without Sherlock and Watson helping them out every time there's a problem."

As I mentioned, it was the following day. Jillian and I were currently sitting in her store's tiny café, located on Cookbook Nook's upper floor. She currently had my hand in hers and, I have to say, was gripping it tightly. Both of us were content to sit in silence as we each contemplated the recent string of events.

"I'd still like to know how that detective lady got her hands on a transcript of my conversation last week. I mean, that happened at Marauder's Grill, and we were sitting outside. Do you know what this means? It means that, somehow, the table where we were sitting was bugged!"

"Or someone sitting nearby could have over-heard," Jillian suggested. "Do you remember if the restaurant was busy that day?"

I thought back to the day in question. We had gone out around 12:30 p.m. The weather was sunny, and I even think that might've been the day I had taken the hardtop off my Jeep. Yes, it was late summer, but I wasn't the type to drive around in hot weather with the top off. Who would want to have a hot hair dryer blasting at you as you drove? Certainly not me.

"It was really nice that day," I recalled. "I'm pretty sure that was the day I took the Jeep's top off. I picked up Vance and Harry, and thought Harry really ought to consider trading in his van, seeing how he wouldn't stop complaining about recent repairs."

"Go on," Jillian urged. "The more you can re-call, the better chance you'll have at remember-ing who might have been out on the terrace with you."

"Well, I walked out, onto the patio. It wasn't too busy, as there was only one waitress assigned to the outdoor tables. But, I do recall someone else. It was a guy, and he was sitting off by himself."

"Did you sit close to him?" Jillian wanted to know.

I shook my head. "No. I mean, the patio isn't that big, and we were only a few tables away. At least, I think we were. Do you think he might've been recording us?"

"I know the owner of Marauder's Grill," Jillian began. "I can..."

"Of course you know him," I chuckled.

"Her," she corrected, with a smile. "As I was saying..."

"Oh, don't tell me," I interrupted for the second time. "Are you part owner?"

Jillian laughed and swatted my arm. "No, of course not."

"Ah."

"My share is less than nine percent."

"Huh? I can't tell if you're being serious or not."

"As I was saying," Jillian repeated, only this time, she dug her nails into my hand, in an unspoken dare, "I can see if anyone there remembers this person's identity. If all else fails, then we could always check their security cameras."

"Sounds like an awful lot of work for something that might be just a fluke," I said.

"It's not a fluke," Jillian assured me. "Someone has it out for you, and I will not sit by and do nothing."

"I'm glad you're on my side," I told her, as I patted her hand. If you're wondering, yes, I could see the crescent-shaped indentations on my skin from where Jillian had latched on.

"No one believes you killed Clara," Jillian assured me, as another ten minutes passed. "Deidra is the best attorney I know. She's good and she's ruthless. I wouldn't be surprised if the charges are dropped by the end of the day."

"Wouldn't that be nice?" I sighed, as I made a point of crossing my fingers in front of her.

"Zachary, let me ask you something."

"Go ahead."

"From what you said, the police department had quite a few quotes from when you were talking about Clara. I think we both know they probably weren't the most favorable."

I waited to see where she was going with this before responding.

"Did you really dislike Clara that much?"

I shook my head. "No, I didn't. It's just that ... hmm, how do I best phrase this without making myself sound like a jerk?"

"Honesty is always the best policy," Jillian assured me.

After a few moments, I shrugged. "All right, let me set the record straight. The only issue I had with her, aside from her colorful wardrobe, was her inability to have a conversation without being in your face. Most people, myself included, don't like it when others violate their personal space. If someone steps too close to you, then you'd be inclined to take a few steps in the opposite direction, am I right?"

"I'm like that," Jillian admitted. "Did something happen that day? The one where you were secretly recorded?"

I thought about it for a few moments before shaking my head. "Not really. I mean, there we were, the three of us, having lunch. The door opens and in comes Clara, only I think she was sashaying toward the counter. I remember looking at the clerk, who was male and young and probably a high-schooler. Anyway, she picks up her order, openly flirts with the cashier, and then sashays out, wiggling her butt the entire time. Seriously, it was a few steps away from being a full-on twerk."

Without missing a beat, Jillian looked me straight in the eye, and asked, "What were you doing looking at her bottom?"

I laughed. "Trust me, I wasn't trying. Neither were Vance or Harry. Oh, man. I couldn't unsee that. Trust me, I've been trying to forget the whole ordeal."

A titter of laughter from a nearby table drew our attention.

Three tables away, near the stairs leading down to the main floor, sat a young woman who looked to be in her mid to late twenties. She wore a bright yellow shirt, ripped blue jeans, and red sneakers. Completing the polychromatic picture was the fact that her blonde hair had streaks of pink and purple running through it. She was staring directly at me and was grinning, as though she and I had just shared some type of joke with one another.

"I'd like to be able to say that I have no idea what that would look like," the young woman told us, "but, unfortunately, I've witnessed it on more occasions than I'd like to admit. No one needs to see something like that. I don't even like it when people my age do it to me."

"Do what?" I asked. "Twerk? Twerking? I don't even know if that's the proper way to say the word."

"Twerk," the girl confirmed, still grinning.

"I'm just thankful Clara Hanson never tried that with me. Good grief, that'd put me in therapy for years."

"Perhaps she knew it'd traumatize you so she never bothered to try?" the girl suggested, giggling.

Jillian laughed. "Zachary would have been horrified."

"I really would," I confirmed.

"And you said she had a colorful wardrobe?" the girl said, after wiping the tears from her eyes with a napkin.

"It was interesting, to say the least," I answered, chuckling. "I ... what's the matter?"

I trailed off once I noticed Jillian's face. She was staring, better make that studying, the newcomer's face. After a few moments, a smile appeared and Jillian began nodding.

"I thought that was you."

"Hello, Ms. Cooper. I was wondering if you'd recognize me. After all, it has been a while."

Confused, I looked at Jillian and waited to see if she'd make the introductions.

"Oh, I'm sorry. This is my fiancé, Zachary Anderson."

The girl rose from her table, approached, and shook my hand, and then returned to her table. Immediately apparent were heavy callouses, proof positive this girl was used to working for a living.

"Zachary," Jillian continued, "may I present Darla Hanson."

I cocked my head. Hanson? Hadn't I heard something about Clara's next-of-kin flying in from San Francisco? Didn't that make her...

"Hello, Mr. Anderson," Darla said, as she grinned at me. "You can call me Dottie. Yes, I'm Clara Hanson's daughter."

"I'm sorry about your mother. You're her daughter? Really? Wow. I wouldn't have called that. I figured you'd be older. Much older."

"I was a surprise," Dottie sadly admitted. "Mom was partying a little too much after her latest husband had passed away. She hooked up with some guy and presto, nine months later, I was born."

I looked at Jillian. "I have no idea how to respond to that."

"I've heard about this," Jillian confirmed. "Sadly, Dottie's father was in the military, and was killed during his last tour."

"Then, I'm definitely sorry to hear that," I offered to the girl.

"You didn't know him," Dottie said. "Neither did I, for that matter. He died before I was born."

"When did you arrive?" Jillian asked.

"I've been in town now for a few days," Dottie told us. "I heard about your arrest, Zachary. Don't worry, I know you didn't do it. You don't seem like the type."

"Thanks. Wait. My type? What is that supposed to mean?"

Dottie shrugged. "Well, I don't want to live in a world where Chastity Wadsworth is capable of murder."

I stared at Dottie with shock written all over my features. "You know I'm an author?"

"I know you're my favorite author."

Jillian clapped her hands, delighted. "How long have you known about Zachary?"

"For a number of years now."

"I clearly didn't do a good job hiding my secret identity," I chuckled. "Nevertheless, thank you for being on my side. At least someone is."

Let me pause here and ask a question. Have you ever said anything so stupid that, once it escapes your lips, you wish you could take it back? Or else whip out one of those little memory messer-upper things from *Men in Black*? I had no sooner uttered those words when I felt a pair of eyes boring into the back of my skull.

"Else. Someone *else* is on my side." I patted Jillian's hand and offered her a smile. After a few moments, when it wasn't returned, I sighed. "All right. How many, and when do you want them?"

"Huh?" Dottie stammered, confused.

Jillian finally smiled. "It's his penalty, for getting out of the doghouse. Since neither of us enjoys arguing or fighting, we decided it'd be much easier to simply agree to get a get-out-jail-free card. What that card turns out to be will depend on the situation. For now, I haven't decided yet. I'll tell you when I do, Zachary. So, Dottie, why did it take so long for you to stop by?"

I felt Jillian's nails slowly rake across my arm on their way to my hand. I tried to inch away, but Jillian was quicker. Just like that, my fingers were entwined with hers. She gave me a quick smile, and then positioned her fingers in such a way where I felt I was being dared to say something snarky again. No thank you, dear. I like my skin right where it is.

"I don't know," the girl admitted. "I guess I just wanted to get a feel for what people really thought of my mother. I wanted to know if anything had changed since I left."

"And has it?" Jillian asked. "I know you and your mother were never that close."

Dottie shook her head, sending strands of pink and purple hair flopping about. "No, not really. Mom's refusal to act her age was one of the main reasons why I left. I just couldn't handle it anymore."

"Did she ever tell you why she did it?" Jillian gently asked.

"Why she acted like a nutjob?" Dottie asked. "Uh, no, not really. She couldn't accept the fact that people were always telling her she was behaving immaturely, and that she should…" air quotes were added here, "…'act her age'. Mom thought she was young at heart, and to hell with anyone who thought otherwise."

"Would you like to join us?" Jillian offered, as she indicated one of the two open chairs at our table.

"You don't mind?" Dottie hesitated. "I've been in town for a few days now, and really haven't had a chance to talk to anyone. I would appreciate it."

"Think nothing of it. Come on over."

The young woman eagerly pushed away from her empty table and practically skipped over to ours. As I looked up at our guest, I couldn't help but feel a little bad for her. Here was someone who was new in town, who didn't have any family, and according to her, there wasn't anyone with whom she could talk. A quick glance confirmed Jillian had already come to the same conclusions, hence the invitation to join us.

"How well did you know my mom?" Dottie asked, as she pulled out a chair. "Based on what you were just saying, I can only assume you knew her well?"

I drummed my fingers on the table and looked

at Jillian as I wondered how much I should say.

"It's okay," Dottie assured me. "I know what she was like."

"Her personality and mine really didn't mix too well," I began. "I will admit, I was running out of excuses when it came to keeping my distance. Each visit to her bookstore was a challenge. I guess I'm just not a fan of anyone who thinks it's socially acceptable to get within an inch or two of your face when having a conversation."

"Mom was always like that," Dottie sighed. "Pleas to maintain a safe distance always fell upon deaf ears."

I looked at Clara's daughter and sighed. "Hey, listen to me a for a second. No matter how much I didn't care to share the same room with her, I never would have wished her harm. I don't even like talking badly about her now when she's unable to speak for herself."

Dottie looked over at Jillian, who nodded.

"And that's why I love this man," Jillian gushed. "Zachary, apology accepted."

I grinned at Dottie and blew Jillian a kiss.

"You two make a great couple," Dottie informed us. "How long have you known each other?"

"A couple of years now," I said. "I moved to town after my wife's accident, back in Arizona. I needed a fresh start."

"That must have been when you wrote the sequel to *On Baited Breath*. Usually, each book you wrote was better than the previous one in the series, but..."

"The sequel stunk," I finished for her, drawing snorts of surprise from both women. "It's okay. I already know it wasn't too good. I can't speak for other writers but as for me, well, my current frame of mind plays an important part in conveying emotions for my characters. If I'm in a lousy mood, then my characters will appear angry, dark. If I'm in a good mood, then the story flows. Everyone is happy. Well, most of the time, at least."

"Your books got me through some tough times," Dottie admitted. "After I moved out of PV, to California, I suffered from depression for several years. Then, one day, I'm sitting by myself in some mall's food court, and I notice the person sitting at the next table over was reading a book."

"One of mine," I guessed.

"*The Ravens of Deveraux Castle*," Dottie said, as she nodded her head. "Up until that point, I've never considered myself much of a reader, and I was certainly not a fan of romance. Umm, no offense. But now? I've always got a few of your books with me, waiting to be read. Thankfully, you've got quite a backlog of titles to choose from. Don't ever stop writing."

"I have no plans to," I assured her, as I placed my hand over hers and gave it a friendly squeeze. "Nowadays, most people are looking for a little bit of escapism in their busy lives. I'm glad I could provide that."

"And you did," Dottie confirmed. She took a sip from her drink and sat back in her chair. After a few moments, she looked over at me and then Jillian. "Do either of you remember much from the day Mom died?"

I softly groaned as I heard this.

Dottie's eyes immediately shifted over to mine. "You know something, don't you? Could you … that is, would you please tell me what happened to her?"

I sighed heavily. "Dottie, I don't know of anyone who would willingly want to know how one of their parents died. You seriously don't want me to tell you that, do you?"

"I do," Dottie whispered.

"Zachary," Jillian quietly began, "it's her mother. She deserves to know."

"Thank…"

"However," Jillian hastily interrupted, "you may not like what you're about to hear."

"…you. You're right. I probably won't like it. That doesn't mean I don't want to hear it. Zachary, please. Please tell me."

Upon finding our table's napkin dispenser missing, Jillian reached across to the neighboring table and snagged theirs. Sliding it over to our guest, my fiancée nodded encouragingly at me.

"Very well. Don't say I didn't warn you. So, what would you like to know?"

"What happened to her?" Dottie quietly asked.

Jillian placed her left hand over mine and her

right over Dottie's. "I'm a firm believer in telling the truth. I always have been. Now, however, I'm having second thoughts. Are you absolutely sure you want to hear this? I'm thinking I should have sided with Zachary."

"I'm no longer a child," Dottie announced, using a faint, faraway voice. "I can take it."

Jillian looked at me. *It's your call.*

I sighed again, shrugged, and then finally nodded. "It would appear that whoever was responsible for your mother's death, well, they wanted something from her. Whether it was information or possibly something else, we don't know."

Horrified, Dottie's mouth dropped open. "Wait, what? She was tortured?"

I paled and looked over at Jillian. Oh, snap. She hadn't known? Jillian's expression, unfortunately, mirrored my own.

"You didn't know," Jillian guessed.

"No, I didn't. Mom was murdered? The police told me she was found in her store, in the backroom. Do we know by whom?"

"We do not," I answered. "It's still an active investigation."

"I don't understand. Mom owned a bookstore. What could she possibly have had that someone would have wanted? I was just in her store earlier today. Trust me, it's just a bunch of old books."

"Your mother loved old books," Jillian softly told her. "They might have been worthless to most people, but she viewed them as treasure, I'm sure."

Dottie took Jillian's hand and clasped it tightly in her own. "I just don't understand. Who would do such a thing?"

Jillian patted Dottie's hand. "We don't know, my dear. You can't let yourself dwell on it. Instead, try to remember all the good things about your mother."

"I know she was found at the bookstore," Dottie sullenly reported. "Does that mean someone killed her in her own store?"

I sadly nodded. "That's what I was told, yes."

"I don't know if I can step foot in that place again," Dottie sobbed.

"Would it help if Zachary and I accompany you?" Jillian offered. "That way, you can see for yourself you have nothing to fear."

Dottie sat, dejectedly, in her chair. After a minute or two of silence had passed, she finally looked up at us. Well, specifically, at Jillian. "I think I'd like that. That is, if either of you don't mind."

Jillian looked hopefully over at me. I nodded, but then remembered something. "I can certainly help out, but I need to run home first."

"You do?" Jillian anxiously asked. "Is everything okay?"

"It will be. I need to pick up their Royal Canineships. It'd be good for them to stretch their legs for a little bit."

As I had hoped, Dottie cracked a smile. "Their

Royal Canineships?" she giggled. "You're going to have to explain that one, please."

"My two dogs," I explained. "They've been cooped up in my house for a few hours now. They could use some exercise."

"What kind of dogs do you have?" Dottie asked.

"Pembroke Welsh Corgis," I answered, with a flourish. "The Queen of England's favorite."

Dottie's face lit up. "Those squat little dogs with short legs?"

"The one and the same," I confirmed.

"I can't wait to meet them," Dottie gushed. "I've always wanted to meet a corgi in person."

"Sherlock and Watson are two of the sweetest dogs you'll ever meet," Jillian assured her. "And, some of the smartest."

"Sherlock and Watson," Dottie repeated. "I love it."

An hour passed. I had just parked my Jeep outside A Lazy Afternoon and had unloaded the dogs. Sherlock promptly shook himself, looked up at the door directly ahead of us, and then looked back at his packmate, as if he couldn't believe Watson wasn't as ready as quickly as he was. Jillian met the dogs at the door and, propping the door open, ushered them both inside. As for me? Well, I was currently wrestling with a large, iron cage I had been suckered into taking home. Gently screwing the base back to the top portion, I offered the occupant a finger. No, not the finger you're probably thinking. Get your mind out of the gutter. I'm talking about my index finger. Once extended, the little gray parrot immediately hopped over and nuzzled my hand. I let the affectionate bird cuddle with me for a few moments longer before I returned her to her cage. As I neared the front door, Ruby began hopping up and down, squawking excitedly.

"Oh, I hope she's not expecting to see Clara," Jillian quietly confided to me.

"She's a smart little bird. She's going to figure it out sooner or later."

Placing the cage back where I had originally taken it, I heard Dottie approach from behind.

"What's this?"

Surprised, I turned to our new friend. "You can't possibly tell me you didn't know about Ruby."

Dottie gazed inside the cage and fell silent.

"She's yours now," I gently announced. "Ruby, this is Dottie. She'll be taking care of you from now on."

I opened the cage door, only to have the little parrot fly straight to my shoulder.

"She seems to like you," Dottie said, as she smiled wistfully at the bird.

Ruby, for her part, flatly refused to even look in Dottie's direction.

"How do you feel about parrots?" Jillian asked, as she joined me and Dottie behind the counter.

"I don't have anything against birds," Dottie hesitantly began, "but I do have to admit that I've never taken care of one before. Look, she likes you so much, Zachary, that perhaps you should take her?"

I pointed down at the dogs, who were both craning their heads up at the cage. "I already have these two. Besides, Ruby belonged to your mother. She belongs to you now, as does the store, I'm sure."

"It does," Dottie confirmed. "I've already met with mom's lawyer. She left everything to me. After how horribly I treated her, she still left me everything. Let's face it. I'm a rotten excuse for a human being."

"Nonsense," Jillian soothingly told her. "Don't worry about Ruby for now. She knows the store. Clara used to let her roam freely. Come on, why don't you let me show you around?"

Dottie nodded and reached into a pocket to pull out a packet of tissues.

***

"I never knew there was so much to running a business," Dottie confided to the two of us, nearly two hours later. "Inventory, sales reporting, and suppliers. It's enough to give me a headache. Did you mean what you said earlier? Will you help me get the store back up and running?"

"If you're serious about staying in Pomme Valley," Jillian said, as she leveled her gaze at Dottie, "then the offer stands. I will help you figure everything out."

"That's so nice of you. I really don't know how to thank you."

"You can thank me by keeping this store open, in your mother's memory," Jillian answered. "It's what she would have wanted."

"I can do that," Dottie promised.

"What about your life back in California?" I asked. "Aren't you going to need to go back there for a while? To close everything up, that is? Put your house up for sale? Put your things in storage, and so on?"

"I was renting a room," Dottie told me. "It was already furnished. None of that stuff was mine."

"Clothes?" Jillian prompted.

"I don't have much. What I have, I brought with me."

"Car?" I asked.

"Don't have one. San Francisco had everything I needed, and it was well within walking distance."

"PV isn't the same," Jillian said. "You're going to need a car, Dottie, or you aren't going to make it very far. I happen to know Clara's house is about three miles from here. One way."

"Ugh. I can't afford a car, Jillian. I barely had enough to scrape together for the flight here."

"It'll be okay," she told the girl. "I know a few people who might have a decent used car for sale."

"But, I just said…"

"Jillian will figure it out," I assured her. "Trust me, she's good at that sort of thing. Now, I was wondering if you'd be able to satisfy my curiosity on something."

Overwhelmed, Dottie could only just stare at me. Eventually, she nodded. "If I can. What can I do for you?"

"Do you have your mother's keys to this place?"

"Yes. The lawyer had them. He was given them by the police. Why? Do you need them for something?"

I pointed toward the back of the store. "There's a door back there, presently locked, and I'm hoping you might have the key for it."

Dottie fished out the keys from her trouser pocket and offered them to me. "You're more than welcome to look. I trust you two more than I trusted my own parents, don't ask me why. Feel free to look around."

Surprised by Dottie's statement of trust, I glanced over at Jillian, who smiled warmly at me. Then, as was often the case whenever my fiancée had promised a favor to another, she pulled out her phone and began tapping the screen. Satisfied she'd be busy for a few moments, I tugged on the leashes and started walking. Both corgis fell into step beside me.

"I'm hoping we'll finally see what's behind door number one," I jokingly told the dogs. "Curiosity kills, doesn't it?"

Sherlock and Watson both glanced up at me, as if they understood the reference. Sherlock snorted, and Watson shook her collar. Standing before the rusty gray door once more, I began trying keys. Since there were only four on the ring, it didn't take long. Sadly, there wasn't a key for this particular door. Where, then, could it be?

"Rats. Foiled again."

"What's the matter?" I heard Dottie call from the counter.

"You don't have a key for this door. It's okay. I'm sure it just leads outside."

"That big, gray door?" Jillian asked. I heard footsteps and decided to wait where I was until she arrived. "I'm sure that doesn't lead outside, Zachary."

Dottie appeared moments later.

"Are you sure?" I asked. "Isn't the alley directly behind this building? I mean, I thought all of these stores had back doors."

"This door is facing the wrong direction," Jillian decided, after taking a few moments to study the sealed door. "This door would have to be facing north, only I'm fairly confident it's facing northeast."

"So, where does it go?" I wanted to know.

Jillian then pointed at the padlock I was still holding. "And, since when are there padlocks securing exterior doors? No, I may not know where that door goes, but I can tell you it doesn't lead outside."

"We'd have to call a locksmith," Dottie decided. "Or, in my case, find someone with a hacksaw."

My eyes lit up and I smiled. "Or, option three."

"Which is?" Dottie curiously asked.

"I pick the lock."

Dottie's eyebrows shot up while Jillian smiled and shook her head.

"You've been waiting for an opportunity to try, haven't you?"

I grinned. "Guilty as charged. Dottie, say the word, and I'll try to get this door open for you."

"Umm, all right. Do you typically carry around a set of lockpicks?"

"No, but I do have a kit back at my house. Jillian? Would you watch the dogs? I'll just run back home."

"Of course. Would you grab something for me?"

"Sure! What do you need? A bottle of water?"

"No, thank you. I'm fine. I was just thinking that, perhaps, you should grab your hacksaw. Just in case."

"Everyone's a critic."

Less than thirty minutes later, I had my tension wrench inserted into the lock, and had just inserted my pick when I noticed I had an audience. Two women, two corgis, and a parrot were all watching me intently. Ruby had returned to Sherlock's back and had promptly created another makeshift nest. Sherlock, surprisingly, didn't seem to have a problem with this. Perhaps he could sense that Ruby was pining for her owner? Regardless of the reason, the two of them were getting along, so who was I to argue? Watson gently sniffed noses with the parrot before returning her attention to me.

"There's the first binder pin," I murmured, as I gently probed with the pick. Encountering the second, I gently pushed the tumbler up, past the shear line. "And there's the second. Hmm, this feels like a five tumbler lock."

"What..." Dottie began.

Jillian placed a finger to her lips. "Shh. Watch. I think Zachary is getting close. If we're lucky, and if he concentrates hard enough, he might stick his tongue out, like Lucy."

"From the Peanuts comic strip," Dottie giggled. "That's hysterical."

"Women," I groaned. "No respect. Ah. There we are."

The rusty padlock popped open. Unhooking the lock, I handed it to Dottie and stepped back out of the way. Dottie started reaching for the door, then she hesitated.

"What if there's a dead body behind this door?"

I looked at Jillian, who helplessly held up her hands in an I-don't-know gesture. Shrugging, I reached for the door and left my hand on the door knob. Seeing Dottie nod her permission, I opened the door to reveal ... stairs.

"There's a basement?" Jillian said, amazed. "Zachary, did you know that?"

"Nope, I did not."

Dottie eyed the dusty, narrow staircase and looked back at the two of us. "If I go down there, will the two of you go with me?"

I nodded. "Sure. Jillian, are you up for a little exploring?"

Jillian smiled. "Why, I'd be delighted, kind sir. Dottie? Would you care to lead?"

"I wouldn't," came the immediate response.

"Well, then, would you do the honors, Zachary?"

"Sure. Would you take the dogs?"

Jillian immediately handed one leash to Dottie. "Would you? I would rather not be pulled down the stairs by two dogs."

"I'd love to," Dottie gushed. She looked down at the red and white corgi and scratched behind her ears. "Which one is this?"

"That's Watson."

"Hello, Watson. I'm pleased to meet you."

Watson returned the greeting by giving Dottie's hand a friendly lick.

"All acquainted?" I asked. "Beautiful. Shall we?"

Carefully leading the procession down the narrow stairs, with my cell phone's flashlight held high over my head, our little group emerged into the shop's tiny basement. There was a light switch within reach and, after I had turned it on, we decided it hadn't been used in decades. The bulb buzzed for a few moments as it reluctantly illuminated, but as it warmed up the noise ceased. Becoming brighter by the second, we were eventually able to view the basement in its entirety.

The room was, perhaps, a hundred twenty square feet. Dusty, decaying cardboard boxes were stacked halfway up the opposite wall. A quick check of the closest box revealed it contained political pamphlets. Advertisements, really. The paper was moldy and the colors weren't too crisp, but it was the same political crap you'd find in your mail during voting season. Did they all contain the same thing?

"This one has a collection of ... of ... what, dishes?" I reported, as I chose a box at random.

Jillian pushed by me to take a look. "Dishes? Oh, wow. You're right. These are gorgeous."

I picked another box. "This one has some type of ceramics in it. More dishes?"

Dottie leaned over my shoulder to take a look.

"Cookie jars! Why, I'd recognize those anywhere. Wow. Some of these might be worth something."

"There's an antique store in town," Jillian began. "Burt, the owner, is a friend of mine. He'd give you a fair price if you allow him first dibs on anything you'd be willing to sell."

Dottie nodded. "Noted."

"Found a box with some newspaper in it," I reported.

"What's the date?" Jillian wanted to know.

"Uh, let's see. Here we go. March 25th, 1968."

"1968," Jillian repeated. "That's the year Clara's father disappeared."

"What are in those crates?" Dottie asked, pointing at the opposite corner.

I wandered over and carefully shone my light

in the closest crate.

"This one has a lantern. Hang on. Yeah, I smell kerosene. This is definitely a lantern. And we have… rope. Looks like it could have come from the sixties, too. Let's see what else we have." I moved to the next crate and found a bunch of hand tools. I selected a few and held them up. "Umm, these are funny little hammers."

"What so funny about them?" Jillian wanted to know.

I passed her several of them. "Well, look at the heads. One is domed. This one is a small, flat square. And this one? It looks like … I don't know. I really don't know what it's for. Dottie? Have you ever seen these before?"

Dottie shook her head no.

"Look over there, Zachary," Jillian instructed, as she shone her light in yet another corner. "Do you see that? Aren't those anvils?"

"Yeah, they are," I confirmed, as I studied one of them up close. "I have no idea what they're doing in the basement of a book store."

Jillian's face turned pensive. "Wait a moment. I think I may know what this stuff is. Let me check something."

"What's she doing?" Dottie quietly asked, as she sidled up next to me.

I pointed at Jillian's phone. "You won't find anyone who's better on a phone than Jillian. She can type out a complex search request faster than it takes me to find the calculator."

"True story," Jillian admitted.

I noticed a dark blue tarp half-concealing a row of boxes. Pulling it away from the wall revealed more tools. This time, there were a few I could identify.

"We've got some sledge hammers over here. I even see one of those gizmos people used to use to stoke the fires in a fireplace."

"I haven't the foggiest idea what you're talking about," Dottie told me. "Can I see? Oh. You're right. I have seen these before."

"You have? I'm impressed."

"That's right. I've seen 'em used in cartoons."

I snorted with amusement. Jillian, overhearing, wandered close. She nodded knowingly at me before gesturing at the wooden device next to the large hammers.

"It's a pair of bellows. Look there, between those two leather handles. Do you see the bag? Or, more precisely, do you see what's left of the bag?"

Now I recognized the contraption. Dottie was right. I have seen them used in cartoons. Strangely enough, never in person.

"No, it can't be."

Jillian and I turned to see Dottie staring into one of the crates. We watched as she gingerly reached in and pulled out what looked like a two-foot long, thin rapier. As she lifted the curious item higher, what I had come to think of as the pommel slid halfway down the blade, and came to a stop. Dottie's mouth curved upward in a smile.

"I haven't seen this thing in ages."

"So, you do recognize this stuff," Jillian said, smiling.

Dottie shook her head. "No, just this. I used to play with this thing all the time as a child."

"Pirates," I guessed.

Dottie grinned at me and nodded. "I always got to be Captain Hook."

"Did you play down here?" I incredulously asked.

"No. Back home."

"Clara's home," Jillian clarified. "Your childhood home, is that right?"

Dottie nodded. "Right. I thought Mom donated all this stuff years ago."

"I wonder if these things once belonged to Charles?" I asked.

"Probably," Jillian decided. "Although, what he's doing with blacksmithing equipment is beyond me."

Dottie and I both turned.

"What was that?" I asked.

"Say that again?" Dottie added, at the same time.

Jillian started pointing at various things in the room. "Anvils over there, various embossing hammers over here, and down there? A collection of sledge hammers. It doesn't add up."

"Blacksmithing," I repeated, as I looked around the room. "Dottie, your mother said Charles held down a wide variety of jobs. Was one of them blacksmithing?"

"I have no idea," Dottie admitted.

I saw Jillian tapping furiously away on her keyboard before she grunted once, with surprise I think, and then looked at the two of us.

"What?" Dottie asked, curious.

"Two things. First, I wanted to tell you that I have sent out some, er, *feelers* out for a car. You won't have to be worrying about not having transportation, I can assure you.

"But..."

"And second, I need to ask you something."

"Er, go ahead," Dottie said.

"Has your mother ever talked to you about Red Dawg's missing gold mine?"

"His missing what?" Dottie repeated.

"His missing gold mine. Your childhood toy? Well, I think Charlie left that here, as a clue."

"A clue for what?" I wanted to know.

"To find Red Dawg's mine." Jillian pointed at the metal spike Dottie was still holding. "That thing? It's a type of candle holder, and it's the only tool in here which isn't related to blacksmithing."

"You have our attention." I pointed at the strange device Dottie was holding. "Would you care to tell us what it is?"

Jillian rotated her phone until we could see the display. "I think it's a Sticking Tommy."

"It's a what?" I asked, as I stared at the strange contraption in Dottie's hands.

"Zachary, it's a piece of mining equipment!"

NINE

T hat is a piece of mining equipment," Jillian repeated. "From the looks of it, one would probably drive that spike into the wall, and do you see that flat piece of metal which has been curled into a tube? That must be where the candle sits."

"Then why does this holder-part thingy move?" I asked, as I slid the metal bracket up and down the spike. "And check out this hook attached to this moving piece. I fail to see why a miner would want the candle to move around like this."

"I always assumed it was busted," Dottie said, as she hefted the spike in her hand. "To be honest, I always thought I must have broken it during one of the many times I used it as a pirate's sword."

"Is it really called a Sticking Tommy?" I asked. After a few moments, I shrugged. "Well, it's not too hard to see why. I mean, look at that thing. I think ol' Tommy got himself stuck with this thing. You know, it'd make a heckuva murder weapon for a future book."

"Oh, Zachary," Jillian giggled. "You're being silly."

"Am I? Come on! I can't be the only person who must have been wondering how something like this got its name. I mean, look at it. Can't you see this Tommy character, whoever he may be, looking like a pincushion?"

"No wonder I like his books," Dottie said, grinning. "He's got a great sense of humor."

"I'm just saying it could..."

I trailed off as I noticed the dogs. Both Sherlock and Watson only had eyes for this Sticking Tommy contraption. I squatted and held the object out, like a peace offering. Both corgis timidly approached, sniffed it, and then snorted.

"What's with them?" Dottie wanted to know.

I grinned. "Well, there's something we haven't told you about the dogs."

Dottie perked up, interested. "Oh? What's that?"

"They solve crimes," Jillian nonchalantly reported. "Whether it's murder, or burglary, or locating a missing fugitive, Sherlock and Watson have proven they're capable of solving practically any crime you throw their way. Last week, it was a missing mass murderer. Several months ago? They put a stop to a couple of teenagers attempting to loot a sunken galleon in Monterey."

"That's impressive," Dottie decided. "If only ...

wait. Wait a moment. They're working on a case right now, aren't they? Are you guys looking into my mother's death?"

"It's highly suspicious," I confirmed. "I discovered the remains of your grandfather on my property and then your mother is killed, in the same week?"

"I want to help."

"We know you do, Dottie," Jillian told the girl. "And believe it or not, you are right now by allowing Zack and the dogs to look around."

"Someone has it in for my family," Dottie said, as she frowned. "I want to do more than simply allow people to walk around my mom's store."

"That would be your store now," Jillian gently reminded her. "Would you really like to help us? You said you remember playing with this contraption as a child. Do you remember anything else about it? Did your mom ever tell you what it was used for?"

Dottie shook her head. "Not that I can recall. Wait. I can remember playing with it one summer, in front of my mom."

"What did she say about it?" Jillian curiously asked.

"Nothing," Dottie said, shaking her head. "It's like she didn't care about it."

"Or, she didn't know," I guessed.

Jillian nodded. "My thoughts exactly. No wonder Clara never messed with these things down here. She must have figured they were her father's and didn't have the heart to throw them away."

I held out a hand. "Dottie? Would you mind if I studied it for a bit? The dogs have taken a liking to it, and I need to figure out why."

Dottie passed the antique metal device to me. "Be my guest. Keep it as long as you need. It's not like I'm going to need it for my next game of pirates."

"With your permission, Dottie," Jillian began, "I'd like to take some of these antiques over to Burt at Hidden Relic Antiques. I know he would love to see some of these things."

"Help yourself," Dottie said, as she waved her arm around the room. "I didn't know any of this stuff was here, so it's clearly not anything I need."

"I have a feeling that, as soon as I show him the first crate, he'll be wanting to call you to arrange a visit down here. Would that be okay?"

"Perfectly fine," Dottie assured us.

"You've mentioned Burt a few times now," I recalled, as I turned to Jillian. "Is everything okay?"

She nodded. "Of course. It's just that... well, I feel bad. I promised Burt a number of antiques from Highland House, only..."

"...only you ended up keeping the majority of them," I finished for her. "I get it. You're trying to make things right. He's not holding this over your head, is he?"

Even if he was, there wasn't a thing I could do about it. Burt had to be the most intimidating individual I had ever encountered. He denies it, but

I could have sworn I've seen him compete on the World's Strongest Man competition I've seen on television. Trust me, he is that big. I mean, his arms are bigger than my thighs!

Jillian nodded. "That about sums it up. I'm just trying to make things right."

"Where are you guys headed to now?" Dottie asked.

Was it me, or did Dottie sound like she didn't want us to leave? Detecting movement in my peripheral vision, I saw that Jillian had looked my way. She must have noted the tone in Dottie's voice, too.

"Well, much to Zachary's chagrin, I'm sure," Jillian began, as she offered me a smile, "we have a few wedding things to go over."

I sighed. I did promise Jillian that we'd check out some wedding sites online. While not my cup of tea, I did enjoy spending time with her, so I just smiled and nodded. I also couldn't help but hear the tiny sigh Dottie had let out. Jillian and I shared another brief look together, and during the split second we locked eyes, a fleeting, silent discussion took place.

What would you say to having her join us? Jillian's asked me. *She's lonely.*

I gave a subtle nod of my head, and was awarded with a beaming smile.

"Dottie, it's awful dark and dank down here. Why don't you come with us? I'm heading back to my place, and I could always use another woman's opinion regarding all things wedding."

Surprised, Dottie nervously glanced over at me. From the expression on her face, I gathered she thought she was interfering with our time together. Well, let's be honest. She was, but it was okay. I could tell Dottie could use some friends, and for some reason, I was getting the impression that our new friend was looking at me and Jillian as though we had just assumed the role of parental figures.

"I, er, don't want to intrude," Dottie hesitantly began. "You don't need some stranger hanging over your shoulder."

"It's okay," I assured the girl. "I don't mind looking at dishes or flatware. But, if you start asking me about flowers, or music, or anything of the sort, I'm telling you both right now, I'm useless." Both ladies broke out in laughter. "So, Dottie? If you could give me a hand in that department, then I would be eternally grateful."

Dottie smiled at me, then at Jillian, and then nodded as though she had just made up her mind.

"I appreciate that. Tell you what. I have an appointment to talk with mom's attorney, and then if the invitation is still open, could I give you a call? So you could come get me? Would that be okay?"

"Perfectly fine," Jillian assured the girl. "That would be perfectly fine. Just let us know when you're ready to be picked up. Here. I've included both of our cell numbers, in case you need to reach either of us."

The two of us headed for the stairs. I was balancing the crate of antiques Jillian had selected on one hand, and tightly gripping the funky-looking candle holder in the other. Holding the leashes tightly in her hand, Jillian turned to look back at Dottie, who was still gazing around the basement with a sad expression on her face.

"Are you coming? It's rather creepy down here. You shouldn't linger."

"I've noticed a few things from my childhood that I'd like to collect. I'm going to poke around for just a bit. Then, I'll go see what the lawyer has to say." Dottie gave us each a pleading look. "Don't start looking at wedding invitations without me, okay?"

I grunted once and returned the smile. "Deal!"

Jillian and I had just made it up the stairs and back into the store proper, when I noticed both dogs had applied the brakes. Jillian looked at the dogs curiously, and then at the cash register, which is what had seemingly caught their attention.

"What is it?" I asked. "What are they staring at?"

"The cash register, I think," Jillian answered. "There's nothing here, you guys. Can we go?"

Neither dog budged. Noticing the imploring look Jillian had just given me, I set the Tommy Sticker thing on the counter, fished out my phone, and snapped a few photos. Exasperated, I waggled my cell in front of the dogs.

"There. I took a few photos. Happy?"

They were. Both dogs calmly rose to their feet, gave themselves a slight shake, and headed for the door.

"Maybe that's what we can do until Dottie arrives," I announced, as I held the door open for Jillian and the dogs.

"What?" Jillian curiously asked.

"All those pictures I keep taking to make the dogs happy. Maybe we could go through some of them?"

"It's a date, kind sir."

"Why thank you, m'lady," I returned, having played this particular game before.

We then heard twin snorts coming from the dogs. Both Sherlock and Watson were head-tilting me, as though I had lost my marbles.

"Dogs. Hang on, guys. Let me load this stuff in the back and I'll help you guys in."

Back at Carnation Cottage, we were just walking in the door, and I had automatically angled to the left, intent on reaching the study, when Jillian pulled me to a stop. She pointed behind me, in the direction of the front entry.

"It's nice outside. Would you like to sit on the veranda?"

"Sure. The dogs love it, and as long as I can pull these pictures up on the phone and we can actually see them, it shouldn't be a problem."

"Oh. I hadn't thought about that. It is bright

outside."

Jillian poured us a couple of glasses of lemonade and, together, we headed outside. Sitting down on the loveseat, I put my left arm around her shoulders and held her tight. She snuggled close and rested her head on my shoulder.

"Tell me, Zachary. What did you think of Dottie?"

"She's a nice girl. I don't think she's as old as I had originally guessed, which was late twenties, or early thirties. That means Clara must have had her later in life."

"I thought about that, too. And, knowing Clara as well as I did, I can only imagine the last thing she wanted was to be saddled with a child. Poor girl."

"Do you get the impression that Dottie seems to be getting a little attached to us?"

"I did. There's a girl who could probably benefit from therapy. I can't even begin to imagine what her childhood must have been like. Thank you for not having a problem inviting her over."

"I like her. She seems nice, down to earth, and..."

"...lonely," Jillian finished. "I agree."

I pulled out my phone. "Okey dokey. We have some pictures. Let's see if I can figure out where to start."

"At the beginning?" Jillian wryly suggested.

"Snot. Okay. Here we are at the park. This was the day after the bones were discovered, I believe.

The dogs were restless, so I thought if I could throw a ball around for them, they would burn off some of that excess energy."

Jillian nodded and offered me a smile. "Smart. What are they looking at? What are you taking a picture of, anyway?"

I shrugged. "I really didn't know. If memory serves, both Sherlock and Watson stopped playing, and started watching the passing cars. They wouldn't budge until I took a few pictures. So, let's see what we have. Here's the first shot, which looks to be D Street. And... we have another shot of the same street."

"Same cars, too," Jillian added.

"Shots three through seven are all of the same thing, only you can see I must have been hitting the button like crazy. That's frustration for you."

"What were you frustrated about?"

I tapped my phone. "The situation, I guess. I mean, how many times have we done this now, and still have not been able to figure out what those two are looking at until the case has been solved? I mean, what was I taking pictures of? Cars! How lovely."

Jillian laughed and swatted my arm. She then noticed I had moved on to the next set of pictures. "That's Pomme Valley Mercantile, isn't it?"

I nodded. "Yep."

"I thought so. I recognize those plants. I wonder why Sherlock and Watson stopped to look at that display? They're only seedlings, as far as I can tell."

"In bright, colorful pots," I jokingly added. "Does that help us? Absolutely not. And next, we have ... more pictures of those little plants. Two more, to be precise. I don't know. It doesn't make sense to me."

"What's after them?" Jillian wanted to know.

"Well, we have ... no, it looks like we're still in the hardware store. See? There's you, in the background."

"And they're looking at seed packets," Jillian thoughtfully observed, as she studied the picture. "Seedlings and seed packets."

I nodded, as if I knew what I was looking at.

"I'm guessing—just guessing—that seeds are somehow involved."

"Silly man, of course they are. The question is, why?"

I shrugged. Swiping my finger across the phone's display, I moved on to the next set of photos. "Brother. I had forgotten I took these."

"What's it of?" Jillian asked, as she leaned close. She saw the picture and her eyebrows lifted. "Abigail Lawson? You took Abigail's picture? Why?"

"I have no idea," I admitted.

"Ah. I think I have it."

"You do?" I eagerly asked. "I'm all ears."

Jillian tapped my phone. "Well, we now know you have a bottom fetish, and in this one, Abigail is walking away from you, so..."

"*Blech!* O-ho say can you seeeeee!!!!!"

Jillian let out a delighted laugh. She then reached over and placed her hand against my forehead. "Zachary, you're blushing! I could fry an egg on your forehead!"

"Am not," I argued. "And no, you couldn't."

That was a lie. Even I could feel the temperature rising on my face. It felt like I was walking outdoors in Phoenix. In the middle of summer.

Retrieving a tissue from her purse, Jillian dabbed at the corners of her eyes before finally turning to me. "Strike a nerve, did I?"

"Yes, Master Yoda," I grumbled, "strike a nerve, you did."

"Oh, I love it. I've never laughed so much in my life. Now, what's next?"

I hastily swiped my finger across the display. Another shot of Abigail's backside appeared. Groaning, I swiped again. Sure enough, a third picture of the retreating Abigail appeared. Before Jillian could comment, I held up a finger and waggled it.

"No, you don't. No comments. Moving on."

Jillian dabbed at her eyes a second time before nodding.

"Okay, here we go. This one was taken at Clara's bookstore."

"Is that one of the displays?" Jillian asked, as she studied the picture.

"Yes. I remember telling the dogs the featured author there had predictable books, whereas mine weren't. For the record, I don't think they were impressed."

"How many photos did you take of the display?" Jillian wanted to know.

"Well, this is the first. Then we have a second, and a third, and a ... hold up. The displays are different. Let me backtrack for a second. Yeah, do you see this? The display changed after the second picture."

"Are the books featuring the same author?"

I showed Jillian the phone. "Umm, there aren't any books on this display."

"You're right. Looks like Clara was featuring some type of local artist. I can see some souvenir keychains, decks of playing cards, and even some candles. What does it mean?"

"Beats me," I admitted. "And ... wow, I don't even remember taking these. How sad is that? Look, there's another display. And a fourth."

"Any books?" Jillian asked.

"Only the first display featured books. The last three has everything but books on them. How is that supposed to help us, I'm not sure."

"Your dogs are something else," Jillian commented. "I had no idea corgis were so smart."

"These could just simply be random pictures," I argued. "Until we know otherwise, we should probably treat them as such."

"Has that ever worked for you?" Jillian argued back. "You've been doing this now for a couple of years. Has Sherlock ever been wrong? Has Watson? You said it yourself when you told me that somehow, inexplicably, whatever the dogs stop to look at will have some type of connection to your case."

"It's just frustrating," I grumbled. I looked at the two corgis, who were both snoozing contentedly on the couch. "Just once, I'd like to be able to figure all this out before they do."

"Based on what I've seen so far," Jillian said, "I don't think that will be happening this time around."

"Thanks a lot," I laughed. "Oh, hey, look! There's a couple more pictures in here."

"What of?" Jillian asked, as she scooted closer to me on the couch.

"Woof!"

We both looked over at Sherlock, who was eyeing us from his upside-down position on the couch.

"Go back to sleep," I told the feisty corgi. "If I want to cuddle next to her, then it's okay. She's not going to hurt me."

"It's true," Jillian added. "I would never hurt your daddy."

Satisfied, Sherlock went back to sleep.

"Protective little things, aren't they?" Jillian observed, with a giggle. "That should make you feel good."

"Well, yes and no," I admitted. "Yes, it means they care, but no in the sense that they don't trust you to be around me. What do they think you're going to do to me?"

"Dastardly things," Jillian giggled. "Is that my greenhouse?"

I looked down at my phone, just before it shut off due to inactivity. Waking it back up, I nodded.

"I remember thinking there must have been something out there that the dogs could smell. Coincidentally, there is."

"And that is?" Jillian curiously inquired.

"Fertilizer, wet earth, and so on."

"And plants," Jillian added, as she pointed at my phone. "Seedlings, seeds, and plants. That's three sets of pictures with a common denominator."

"And finally, we have the picture I took earlier today."

"From today? Very well, I'll bite. What can you see?"

"Clara's cash register."

"Oh, that's right. I had forgotten about that one. Well, can you tell what the dogs are looking at?"

I nodded. "Yes, I sure can. It's the cash register."

Jillian laughed, and took the phone so she could study the picture herself. After a few minutes had passed, she sat back.

"Well?" I prompted.

"If there's something else in that picture, then I can't tell what it is."

"No plants, or anything of the sort?" I asked.

"No plants. I don't know how this picture fits in."

"And the others?" I prompted. "Any idea how

they fit in?"

"I really don't know. I'm sorry."

"Hey, don't be," I soothed. "I appreciate the help."

Both dogs were suddenly wide awake and on their feet. Jillian and I stared at the two of them for a moment or two, but before either of us could say anything, a cell phone began ringing. It was Jillian's.

"Hello? Hi, Dottie. No, you didn't catch me at a bad time. Is everything all right? What? No, wait a moment. Slow down. What's the matter? Do you know what? Let me put you on speakerphone. Zachary is here, too."

"I'm so sorry to dump this on you, when I barely know you," Dottie's voice sobbed out, as Jillian activated the hands-free option. "You've been so nice to me, and I didn't know who else to call."

"Dottie? It's Zack. Listen, are you okay? Are you safe?"

"Hi, Zack. Yes, I'm sorry to freak you guys out. I … I think I was just suddenly swamped with emotion. I felt like I needed to talk to someone."

"Don't apologize," I told the girl, which earned me a smile from Jillian. "I'm just making sure you're safe. What's going on? Can you tell us?"

"I … oh, it's stupid. I really shouldn't be bothering you guys with this."

"Dottie, nothing is stupid," Jillian firmly stated. "You've been going through a lot. If something happened, then please let us help."

"Thank you, Jillian. It's just that … well, I was poking through some of that stuff in the basement. I should have just left it alone, but no. I had to be nosey."

"You found something," I guessed.

"A bundle of letters from my mom," Dottie answered. "She kept the letters I had sent back. I guess … I guess my mother didn't hate me after all."

Jillian reached out and tapped her cell phone's display. "It's muted. Would you be willing to go back to the bookstore? The poor girl is so emotional right now, and she shouldn't be alone."

In answer to Jillian's questions, I looked at Sherlock and Watson, who were still awake—and upright—and jingled my keys. "Who wants to go for another ride?"

Twenty minutes later, we were back in the bookstore. Dottie had gone straight to Jillian and wrapped her arms around her, sobbing uncontrollably. Thankful I was excluded, I took the dogs for a quick check of the store's interior. Once more, we made four stops, and it was the same four we had stopped at the last time we did a thorough walk-through of this place. Shrugging as we passed each display, I could only look at the dogs and wonder what was going on in their heads. I checked each of the displays a second time, and found nothing to warrant a second look.

As we approached the counter, where Jillian

and Dottie were still embracing, Sherlock and Watson surprised me again by perking up. Placing ourselves before the cash register, I could see that something up on the counter had attracted their attention, only I had no idea what. Clara's counter, like most retail shops, had a plethora of items scattered across every square inch of its surface. So, that meant the dogs could be looking at this chewing gum, or those candy bars, or perhaps that baseball cap hanging on the wall. Until I found someone who spoke corgi, I was never going to know.

"Feeling better now?" I heard Jillian ask.

Turning, I saw Dottie reluctantly pull away from her. The new shop owner saw me nearby, blushed, and finally nodded. She reached behind the counter, fumbled around a moment or two, and then plunked something down.

"Are these the letters you were telling me about?" Jillian asked.

"Yes. Man, it serves me right. Last week, I thought my life was fine. Everything was going my way, I was living the way I wanted to, and now?"

"You're overwhelmed," Jillian gently explained. "It's to be expected. Your mother passes away..."

"...is murdered," Dottie angrily interrupted.

"...murdered," Jillian reluctantly corrected, "and you are startled to learn you're now a business owner. Plus, your mother undoubtedly left you her house."

Dottie nodded. "She did, yes."

"This will all take time to process. In the meantime, would you like some help going through these letters?"

"You don't mind?" Dottie anxiously asked.

"Not at all. Here. I'll take this chair, and you take the stool, on the other side of the counter."

"Better get used to it, huh?" Dottie quipped, as she offered the two of us a smile. "I just hope I can do this."

"You can," Jillian assured the girl. "And, we're here, in case you need help."

Dottie looked over at me, as if she wasn't sure if Jillian could speak for me. I gave her a subtle nod and an encouraging smile. Emboldened, the two of them started sifting through the stack of envelopes.

"These are all letters that your mom sent to you?" I asked, as I sidled close to Jillian and looked over her shoulder. "So, I take it these are the ones you answered?"

Dottie sadly shook her head. "I answered maybe one letter, two max. And that was years ago. I've never read these before. I started on the first few and, before I knew it, I had begun bawling like a schoolgirl. I mean, what the heck? I'm an adult. Why should I let this bother me?"

As the ladies worked their way through the pile, and Dottie concurrently worked her way through a box of tissues, the dogs and I were content to wander the store. Ruby, who had been confined to her cage, chirped excitedly as she watched me approach. When I released the latch on the cage door, the African gray parrot hurriedly flew to my shoulder, as if she couldn't believe her good fortune.

"Hey there, little girl," I said, as I stroked the bird's head. "How are you holding up?"

"Give us a kiss, Precious! Give us a kiss!"

Finding an armchair near the front of the store, I decided to give my aching feet a break. Seeing me settle down in one place, both dogs circled once and laid down next to me. Ruby watched the dogs for a few moments before she hopped down the length of my arm, across the arm of the chair, and down the length of Sherlock's back. Once she had reached the tri-colored corgi's neck, the little parrot fluttered her wings a few times as she nestled deep into the soft fur.

Sherlock, for his part, never bothered waking up.

Nearly twenty minutes later, with me threatening to doze off in the chair, an exclamation drew me up short. It also woke the dogs, and that was when Sherlock noticed he had a rider on his back. Preparing for the worst, I was ready to snatch the bird off of Sherlock's back, only much to my surprise, Sherlock gave the bird a soft snort and went back to sleep.

"Good job, pal," I told the corgi as I stroked the fur between his ears, which was one of his favorite places for me to scratch. "Ruby doesn't need any more aggravation right now."

"Zachary!" Jillian called. "I think you should come see this!"

"What is it?" I asked, as I rounded the aisle and stopped beside her. "Did you find something?"

Dottie nodded excitedly. "We think so. We found a letter, from Mom, which talks about one of her husbands."

Unsure if I should be excited, I nodded. "Okay. Umm, do we know which one?"

"That part, we're not sure of," Jillian reported, as she skimmed the paper before her. "As near as we can tell, it was just after her most recent husband had passed away. I think Clara was lonely. Her letter is lengthy, at nearly ten pages long."

"Front and back," Dottie sighed. "Mom could get a bit long-winded at times."

"Only a bit, huh?" I softly snorted. "What has you two so excited?"

"Because," Dottie proudly exclaimed, "there's a mention of Red Dawg. Now, I didn't know who he was but Jillian did."

"You found a letter in which Clara mentions Red Dawg?" I incredulously repeated. "By name?"

Jillian nodded. "Yes. Listen to this. She says that Ronald, which must have been the name of her late husband, admitted to knowing Charles, her first husband. Ronald, according to Clara, says he admitted the only reason he married Clara was to search for something."

"Mom was in a full-blown rant," Dottie added.

"On and on she went, for nearly four pages."

Jillian nodded. "Right. At the end of the rant, she said Ronald admitted he knew the lost mine was in PV and that it was hiding in broad daylight. However, he couldn't find it."

"Hiding in broad daylight," I thoughtfully repeated. "What could that mean?"

"I would think that it means that we've probably laid eyes on the mine multiple times," Jillian said, "and didn't know what we were looking at."

I nodded. "Oh, I get it. Like, perhaps, the mine is disguised as something else?"

It was Jillian's turn to nod. "Clever. The question I have is, if the mine is in PV then where is it?"

"What if it was in the city this whole time?" I suggested. "I mean, everyone always assumed that the mine was located somewhere in the outskirts of town. But, what if it wasn't?"

"Well, if it was hidden," Jillian slowly said, "then whatever is disguising it would have to be old."

"How old?" Dottie wanted to know.

I did a quick search on my phone. "1850. It says here that the Oregon State Gold Rush started in 1850, so it'd have to be around that time."

"That's a hundred-seventy years ago," Dottie exclaimed, amazed.

"That's just the start of it," I reminded her. "We already know Red Dawg traveled between PV and Yreka, California, for years. The only problem is, we don't know when he stopped."

"Or, when he was killed," Jillian somberly added. "Let's face it. Any prospector who flaunts his gold, like Red Dawg was said to, was just asking for trouble."

"Red Dawg," Dottie repeated. "Is that the guy who owned the mine we're looking for?"

"Yep," I confirmed, as I turned to the girl. "Why?"

"Well, now that I think about it, I seem to remember seeing that name in one of the earlier letters, too."

Jillian gasped as I suppressed the urge to let out a less-than-gentlemanly exclamation.

"Where? Could you find it again?"

"Sure, I guess. Let me see."

While Dottie searched through the bundle, I glanced down at the dogs. You'd think I had put them through a marathon, as they were out cold. Again.

"Here it is. Look. Mom was going off on Ronald again. She said Ronald wouldn't shut up about some guy named Jake Wellington. Apparently, Jake had red hair, a thick beard, and torn-up hands. He drank too much, cussed too much, and spent money like it was going out of style."

"Hmm," I thoughtfully nodded. "Interesting. Anything else?"

Dottie returned to the letter. "Just a little. It says here that Ronald kept referring to this Jake Wellington person as 'RD', and it drove my mother nuts. Ronald, even though he was repeatedly asked, never let the matter drop."

"RD?" Jillian repeated. "As in, Red Dawg?"

I snapped my fingers. "Mr. Halloway! Do you remember what he said to us?"

"It was something about Charlie finding a key," Jillian answered.

"No, not that. It was after that."

"Then I don't, I'm sorry."

"Derrick Halloway said he believed Charlie had uncovered Red Dawg's identity."

"Jake Wellington?" Jillian asked.

"Think about it," I urged. "This Jake Wellington person has red hair, a red beard, messed-up hands, and he loved to drink. Does that sound like anyone we know?"

"Red Dawg was rumored to spend a lot of time in bars and taverns," Jillian recalled.

"He was always buying drinks for everyone," I reminded her, "and paying for it with gold from his mine. And, this Jake person had messed-up hands, like a miner would."

Jillian pulled her phone out and started researching online. After a few minutes, she gave up. "I can't find anything about a Jake Wellington in PV's history."

"That doesn't mean he isn't Red Dawg," I pointed out.

"But, I did find one mention of a David Wellington."

"Oh? What about him?"

"Well, the Wellington family ran the general

store," Jillian reported. She was furiously scrolling, swiping, and tapping her phone. "No, that's all I can find. One obscure mention of the family name."

"Wellington," I repeated. "Hmm. If they ran the store, and it was the only one in town, then it stands to reason they probably had more than one penny to rub together."

Jillian shrugged. "I'll buy that. What about it?"

"Well, let's assume a few things. First, if Jake Wellington is Red Dawg, and Jake came from this Wellington family, then we know they lived in town."

"We do?" Dottie asked, confused. "Where does it say that?"

Jillian smiled. "It's inference. If you are running a business, and your sole livelihood rests with that store, then you're not going to want to live too far from it, are you?"

"Does it say where the store was?" I eagerly asked.

Jillian shook her head. "No, it doesn't, I'm afraid."

"So, Jake Wellington lived in town. And, he had a gold mine to hide. What would be the easiest way to do that?"

Jillian returned to her phone and typed out a new search. After a few moments, she must have found something surprising, because her eyes widened, and her eyebrows shot up.

"What is it?" I asked, curiosity piqued.

"Well, I'll be. I didn't know that."

"What?" both Dottie and I echoed.

"Zachary, when you think of a mine, what's the first thing that comes to mind?"

I scratched the side of my head. "Are you referring to what it would look like?"

Jillian nodded. 'Yes."

I shrugged. "That's easy. You see a dark, forbidding opening at the base of a mountain."

Jillian looked at Dottie. "And you?"

"I'm with him," Dottie answered, as she pointed at me. "Movies and television shows usually depict a mine as a cave in a mountain."

"What about a hillside?" Jillian challenged.

"I guess so," I decided.

"Well, did you know there's another type of mine called a pit mine?"

"Seeing how I don't really know anything about mining to begin with," I began, "then I'd say it wouldn't be too surprising. What about it?"

"What kind of a mine is that?" Dottie wanted to know. "Is that like the name suggests? You just dig a pit and presto, instant mine?"

"According to its definition, pit mining is a mining technique used when whatever materials you're looking for are found near the surface."

I nodded. "Makes sense. What about it?"

Jillian took my hands in hers and squeezed them tight. "Don't you get it? What if Red Dawg's mine was, in fact, a pit mine and the reason no one has found it is because it was small?"

"So small that it could be easily hidden," Dottie added.

"Like, could-be-hidden-inside-a-house small?" I slowly asked, as a smile formed on my face.

Jillian nodded excitedly. "Yes!"

"But, there aren't any houses that old," I protested.

"True," Jillian admitted, "but we don't need them to be that old. Remember, Red Dawg, or Jake Wellington, I guess, traveled between this area and Northern California every winter. We don't really know when he stopped making that journey. He could have kept his house up-to-date during that time."

"So, the house we're looking for might not be as old," I decided. "But, it'll still be older than everything else around it."

Jillian stiffened with surprise. "Like, say, a historic house?"

"Aren't there a bunch of them here?" I asked, growing excited. "I mean, there's your Highland House, and ... and ... shoot. I don't remember any others."

"You'd need a tourist map for that," Dottie said. "All towns have them. In fact ... in fact, I think I've seen some."

Jillian and I stared at the girl.

"Do you remember where?" Jillian asked.

Dottie nodded. "Yes. It was next to the cash register."

As one, both Jillian and I looked down at the

dogs. Haven't they eyed the cash register on more than one occasion? Sherlock and Watson, sensing the excitement emanating from the three of us, let out enthusiastic barks.

"There they are!" Dottie exclaimed.

I snatched one of the maps out of the clear, acrylic holder they were all resting in, and unfolded it. A street-level map stretched out before me, pinpointing locations of parks, stores, hotels, and so on. Also listed on the map were the locations of Pomme Valley's collection of historic houses.

"There's ten of them," I reported. "It doesn't say how old they are."

Jillian took my hand. "Zachary, one of those houses is hiding Red Dawg's lost gold mine! I just know it!"

TEN

W e had just stepped outside of A Lazy Afternoon, with Jillian and I each holding a leash, when the two of us turned to look back at the store. Dottie was there, standing in the open doorway, with a forlorn smile on her face. I didn't even need to ask my fiancée's permission.

"Well, are you coming or not?"

A wide grin split the girl's face as she eagerly leapt out of the store, turned to lock the door, and hurried over to Jillian's SUV.

"Thank you," the girl whispered, as she hugged Jillian.

"You're welcome. Something tells me you're going to love living here."

I tried slipping into the driver's seat, but not before Dottie hooked my arm and pulled me in for a hug, too.

"Thanks for thinking of me."

"It's what friends do," I told her, as I gave her back a few pats. "Come on. Wanna see if we can find this mine?"

"Like you wouldn't believe."

"As Zachary mentioned," Jillian slowly began as we drove away, "there are less than a dozen historic houses scattered throughout town. Obviously, we can rule out Highland House. Trust me when I say we've been through that house so many times that, had there been a concealed mine, then I know we would have found it."

"And Carnation Cottage," I added. "For obvious reasons."

Jillian smiled and nodded.

"Let's just start with the closest," I decided.

"Very well. The closest one would be Bartlett House. It's off of 5th and Oregon."

"Got it. We'll be there in just a few minutes."

It was definitely not Bartlett House. The building was in pristine condition, the grounds were beautifully landscaped, and there was a steady stream of people going in and out of the door. Why? Well, it looked as though the building was owned by the city and that it was a payment drop-off location for quite a few utilities.

Next up was Prescott House, which was located off of C Street on the western side of town. We knew that wasn't the one, since it was in better shape than Bartlett House. There was no way that much work could be done on a house without discovering a concealed mine. It couldn't be the one.

For the next several hours, the three of us, five if you count the corgis, explored the town. We ended up driving by each of the ten houses several times, and it wasn't until Dottie pulled out her phone and started snapping photos, did we decide to stop for a bite to eat. Sitting down at Casa de Joe's outdoor terrace, we ordered lunch while we compared notes.

"Of the ten houses," Jillian began, "how many would you say are potential candidates?"

"At least half, right?" I guessed.

"I counted four," Jillian argued. "Which ones do you have on your list?"

I unfolded the map we had acquired from A Lazy Afternoon and studied the locations we visited.

"Well, I only thought there were two viable choices."

"Which ones?" Dottie wanted to know, as she munched on a chip.

I tapped the map. "This one, on the corner of C and 4th. The other one I thought would work would be on 6th and D Street."

"I thought that one was too far away," Jillian said, after taking a sip of her iced tea. "I believe Windsor is a strong contender."

"Windsor," I repeated, as I returned to my map. "Let's see."

"It's right there," Dottie said, placing a finger off of Pine Street in the southwestern corner of Pomme Valley.

I peered at the house's location and frowned. "Wouldn't this one be considered too far away, too? I mean, downtown is over here."

"That might not have been downtown for the people living in the 19th century," Jillian helpfully pointed out.

"Oh. That's true. I just wish we could find some indication where the Wellington family's general store was located. I think it'd help us quite a bit."

"I've been searching for it," Jillian admitted. "Thus far, I haven't had much luck."

"Same here," Dottie informed us. "I figure someone, somewhere, must know where it was."

"What are you looking for now?" I asked, as I tapped a chip on our new friend's phone.

"I'm searching for modern-day descendants of the Wellingtons," Dottie answered.

"Any luck?" Jillian hopefully asked.

"No, I'm sorry."

Our lunches were served, a few bowls of water were placed for the dogs, and our own drinks were refilled. Jillian had taken several bites of her grilled chicken chimichanga when her eyes widened. I watched her eyes drop to the map, which was currently folded up and situated by my left elbow. Jillian pointed at the map and held out a hand.

"What is it?" I asked, as I gave her the map. "Did you think of something?"

Jillian pulled out her phone. "I did. I can't believe I didn't think of it earlier."

She fell silent as she pulled up several search engines on her phone.

"What's she doing?" I heard Dottie quietly ask.

"She's got something up her sleeve," I whispered, as I gave Dottie a grin. "We're just going to have to wait to see what it is."

The dogs suddenly perked up and fired off several warning woofs. The three of us looked up just in time to see a bright, neon yellow sub-compact car go driving by. I carefully watched the dogs, seeing how I was intent on discovering what they were watching. Sure enough, as soon as the tiny car hit the next intersection, it made a left-hand turn and disappeared from sight.

Both dogs immediately settled back down.

"That was peculiar," Jillian commented, as she returned to her phone.

"Yeah, it was," I agreed.

Sherlock and Watson were interested in a tiny yellow car? I suddenly thought back to the first set of pictures I had taken for this case and reached for my phone. Could it be? And there it was, in plain view: a sharp yellow car, driving past me on Oregon Street. I checked the next several pictures and discovered this same car was in those shots, too.

"What does it mean?" I quietly mumbled to myself.

"What is it?" Dottie asked, after she caught me frowning.

"Just now? The dogs woofed at that ugly-looking yellow car. Did you see it?"

Dottie nodded. "Yes. What about it?"

I slid my phone over to her and tapped the

screen. "Check this out. The dogs had me take a picture of that car earlier."

Jillian looked up. "What about that yellow car?"

I pointed at my phone. "Remember the set of pictures from the park? Well, that yellow car was in them."

"Really? Did you get a look at the driver?"

"No, I'm afraid not," I admitted. "If I see it again, then please believe me when I say I will do my darnedest to get a shot of the driver."

"I've got her number," Jillian announced. "I thought for certain I had it in my phone, but I don't. I must have accidentally deleted it."

"Whose number?" I curiously asked.

"Devon's. Devon Rice? She runs a local real estate brokerage."

"I doubt very much they're up for sale," I pointed out.

Jillian shook her head. "They don't have to be. Realtors have access to tons of information about houses, including age, size, square footage, and so on. I'm going to see if Devon will help us out by telling us if she can see how old these houses are. Perhaps it will help us?"

"It's a good idea."

"Hello, may I speak with Devon, please?"

Jillian paused as the person on the other end of the line, who I'm guessing was a receptionist, inevitably told her the individual she was looking for was unavailable.

"Yes, I know she's busy. Perhaps you could ... your voice mail is down? Interesting. Then can you take down a message for me? Excellent. Yes, tell her that Jillian Cooper would like to ... oh! She's available? How convenient. Sure, I'll hold."

I looked at her and grinned. "Do you, er, have any clout at that office?"

Jillian returned my smile. "Maybe. Devon, hello! Yes, it's good to talk to you, too. Listen, I have a favor to ask. Are you aware of the ten properties currently registered as historic houses here in PV? Good. I ... no, I'm not currently interested in buying any others, thank you. Listen, I'm trying to figure out which ones are the oldest. It's a bet Zachary and I have. Yes, that Zachary. Yes, he's my fiancé. Sure, I'll hold again."

"You're thinking the oldest must be the one we're looking for?" Dottie quietly asked.

Jillian nodded. "Something along those lines. If any of the historic houses are less than one hundred years old, then I'd say we can probably write them off the list. We've already checked all ten, and you will admit that there are some strong contenders. However, I'd like to scrub our list against the one Devon gives us, and hopefully, it'll give us a direction to go."

"And if it doesn't?" Dottie helplessly asked.

"Then we're no better off than we are now," Jillian answered, with a shrug. "If nothing stands out, then ... what's that? Yes, Devon, I'm still here. You've got the information I need? Thank you so much. Sure, you can email it to me. I can make that work. I ... what's that? Oh, if you have time, I would appreciate it."

Jillian muted the call, looked at me, and then pointed at my jacket.

"Zachary, would you be willing to take some notes?"

I fished my small notebook out and clicked my mechanical pencil a few times and nodded my readiness.

"Go ahead, Devon. We're ready. All right, which one is the oldest? Windsor? That helps, thank you."

I began taking notes.

"Then, in order from oldest to newest," Jillian slowly said, "is Center, then Garden, and then Highland."

I scribbled on, writing as fast as I could.

"After Highland is Laramore, then Willow, and then Bartlett," Jillian intoned, speaking slowly. "And finally, there's Prescott, Carnation, and Mitchell. Thank you so much, Devon. I... what? The ages? Sure, if you have them handy, I'll take them."

I slid my notebook over to her and she proceeded to add the ages to each of the houses listed. Once finished, she thanked her friend and hung up.

"Now what? How does that list compare to the one you made?"

Jillian retrieved the notes she took while we were driving around town and placed the napkin next to my notebook. "Windsor appears to be first on the list."

Dottie handed me the map and I placed a circle around the tiny square denoting Windsor House.

"I had Willow down," Jillian continued, "but according to Devon, Willow is one hundred. One hundred and one, to be precise."

"That's still old," I commented.

"True, but these others are older."

"Which one was the next oldest? Center? How old is that one?"

"One hundred nineteen."

"Wow," Dottie breathed. "Do people actually live in these houses?"

Curious, I turned to Jillian, who shook her head. "No. In order to become livable, the houses would have to be brought up-to-date with current safety regulations, codes, and so on. It's possible, but expensive."

"She just did it with Highland House," I added, as I tapped the square on the map representing Jillian's last investment. "And it wasn't cheap. She turned it into a B & B."

"Nice. Any takers so far?"

Jillian nodded. "As a matter of fact, Highland House is booked through Halloween, and will probably be booked through Christmas shortly."

Finished studying her notes, Jillian looked up. "I'd say we have three strong contenders. Highland House, while being old enough, is going to be ignored. We already know there's nothing there."

Dottie nodded. "Got it. So, what are the three?"

"Windsor, Center, and Garden."

I sighed and leaned back in my chair. "Nice. That definitely narrows it down for us. So, how can we get in there to take a closer look? Can your friend at the real estate place help us out?"

"You heard her. Those houses aren't for sale, so none of the Realtors would have access to it."

"Crud. Hmm. There's gotta be a way."

"Well, I just thought of something we could do."

"Oh, yeah? What's that?"

Jillian pulled out her phone. "I have an idea. Let me make a phone call."

"How many times a day does she charge her phone?" Dottie quietly asked me.

I gestured to Jillian's purse. "See the cord snaking out of the top? Her purse has a built-in charger. But, to answer your question, it averages between two to three times daily."

"Wow."

"Her *life* is that phone. Everyone she needs to be in contact with is on that phone."

"Debra? Hi! It's Jillian Cooper. How are you today?"

I glanced down at Jillian's phone and started to look back up when the name caught my eye: D Campbell. Plus, I had just heard her address this person by Debra. D Campbell, as in Debra Campbell, current mayor of Pomme Valley?

My eyes widened as I realized Jillian was pulling out all the stops. Then, they widened even further as I saw her tap the hands-free option, so that the two of us could hear the conversation.

"Jillian! So sweet of you to call. What can I do for you, my dear?"

"Debra, are you familiar with the historic houses here in town?"

"I am. I'm the one who granted permission for you to purchase Highland House, remember? What can I do for you? Are you interested in another historic house?"

"In a fashion," Jillian admitted. "I need to be able to see inside Windsor House, Center House, and Garden House. Is there any way you could give me permission to do so?"

"Windsor, Center, and Garden. Let me think."

"We were interested in their construction and just wanted a chance to look around."

"I'm sorry, Jillian, dear, but those houses are treasures in the eyes of PV. I can't authorize anyone to enter those houses who doesn't own them."

I made a quick slashing motion across my throat. Jillian immediately muted the call.

"What is it?" she worriedly asked.

"Why were you allowed to purchase Highland House?"

"Well, the city needed the money, I believe."

"And does it now?"

"What, need money? What city doesn't?"

I pointedly looked at the list of house names Jillian was holding and cocked my head. Then, to seal the deal, I gave her a goofy smile. Comprehension dawned. Jillian leaned forward to unmute the call.

"Debra, what if we were to buy those three houses?"

Dottie's eyes opened wide with shock.

"What was that, my dear?"

"What if I renovate those three houses like I did to Highland House?"

"Are you telling me you'd restore those three wonderful houses to their full glory just so you would be able to inspect them up close?"

Jillian nodded. "I would, yes."

"Well, you certainly don't mess around, do you?"

Jillian smiled. "I try not to, ma'am."

"Can I put you on hold?"

"Of course."

"I'm sorry," I immediately apologized. "I should have asked you first. I know this is going to be expensive."

"I can handle it, Zachary. I'll be more than happy to do this for the city."

"Just to look for a lost gold mine?"

"Well, there's that, but to me this feels like the right thing to do."

"You know I'll help."

"Thank you, Zachary. That's very sweet of you but I can handle this."

"You take Windsor and Center," I continued, ignoring her protest, "and I'll take the last one. Garden, I think I heard you say."

"Really, I'll be just fine handling all three by myself."

I looked over at Dottie. "Wasn't that nice of her? Allowing me to take one of the restorations while she handles the other two?"

"But ... but she didn't say it was okay!" Dottie sputtered.

I turned back to Jillian. "It's settled. You'll get two, and I'll get one."

Jillian awarded me her million-dollar-smile and simply shook her head. "And that's why I..."

"Okay, I'm back."

"...love you, Zachary," Jillian finished.

"Am I interrupting something?"

Jillian's face reddened. "I'm sorry, ma'am. My fiancé was just telling me how, should you approve my request, he'll handle one of the restorations while I handle the other two."

"That's right, I had heard you were engaged. Congratulations, my dear! Who's the lucky man? Did you say his name was Zachary?"

"That's right, ma'am. Zachary Anderson. He's the owner of Lentari Cellars."

"And that's why I know the name," Mayor Campbell chuckled. "Very well, my dear. Provided neither you nor your fiancé have plans to ... what do they call it? Flip the house? As long as you don't plan on reselling them for a large markup, consider them yours."

"Thank you, ma'am. Debra. Umm, can I ask

where we can go to pick up keys?"

"Stop by my office. I'll have my assistant pull the keys for you."

"Thank you, Debra."

"No, thank you, Ms. Cooper. Tell your fiancé Pomme Valley thanks you for all your work. I look forward to meeting him at the wedding."

"Yes. Yes, of course."

"You have picked a date, have you not?"

"I, er…"

"I'm just teasing you, my dear. I look forward to meeting your lucky man."

My eyes widened and I nudged Jillian, grinning like a fool as I did so. She smiled, shook her head, and held a finger to her lips.

"I do, too. Again, thank you very much."

Once the call was over, Jillian and I looked at each other and burst out laughing. Well, that was certainly one way to get permission.

"I don't believe you two!" Dottie exclaimed. "Did I hear that right? You guys have to renovate three old houses now? Do you know how much money that's going to cost?"

Both of us nodded.

"Wow. I think I'm in the wrong line of work."

I was about ready to crack a joke when my eyes fell upon Jillian's napkin. Wordlessly, I picked it up and stared at the names.

"What is it?" Jillian asked, concerned.

"I don't believe it. I think I figured it out."

"You've figured what out?" Dottie asked.

I looked up and smiled at both of them. "Oh, this is making so much more sense now! I know where it is. I know where to find Red Dawg's lost mine!"

ELEVEN

W hat is starting to make so much more sense now?" Jillian asked, confused.

I looked back at my two dogs (in the mirror) and shook my head. "Guys? I have no idea how you do it. I owe you guys a trip to the pet store so you can get your favorite treats."

"What's going on?" Dottie asked.

"I'm honestly surprised I didn't notice any of this earlier," I offered, by way of explanation.

Jillian smiled. "Would you care to share, Professor?"

I handed her the napkin she had taken notes on and grinned. "What's the common denominator with the pictures taken at the hardware store and the ones taken at your place? With that in mind, look at the names of the houses and tell me what you think."

Jillian's lovely face looked down at the napkin she was holding and, just like that, her face lit up. She turned to the two dogs, currently sitting in the back seat with Dottie, and ruffled their fur. "Aren't you two the smartest doggies in the whole world?"

I think Sherlock drooled while Watson wriggled with excitement. The reason I know this is that Jillian immediately went for the napkin supply, stored in the glovebox.

"Heap the praise, expect the drool," I chuckled. "And, for the record, I think I should have been able to figure this out a long time ago, too. Well, by *long*, I mean four or five days ago."

"What'd I miss?" Dottie asked, confused. "Zachary takes one look at your napkin and announces he knows where we need to look? How? Where are we going?"

"Show her my phone and the pictures," I said, as I turned onto Main Street. We had just picked up the keys to all three of our new houses and were now on our way to what I had hoped would be the house which had been hiding the mine for over a hundred years.

"That'd be too hard," Jillian informed me. "Let me sum it up. Dottie, these two dogs have the ability to zero in on clues that aren't apparent to everyone else. For example, several days ago, when Zachary and I were in the hardware store, Sherlock and Watson stopped at a display of plants."

"Plants in a hardware store isn't too surprising," Dottie stated.

"True," Jillian said, nodding. "But, these plants

were seedlings; young herb plants. I know, because I went back and zoomed in on the picture. Dill, rosemary, thyme, and so on."

"What does that have to do with...?"

"Let me finish. After the seedlings, the corgis then pulled Zachary over to a display of seeds. This time, they were all vegetables."

"I'm still not following," Dottie helplessly stated.

"A day or so later, Sherlock and Watson wanted to go outside at my house and check out my new greenhouse. What do I have in there? The same thing: plants intended for my garden."

Dottie looked over at me and gave me a pleading look. "I'm feeling so dumb right now. Please tell me, what am I missing?"

"Garden," I repeated. "The dogs have expressed interest in all things *garden*."

"So?"

Jillian handed Dottie the napkin on which she had taken notes. "Of the ten historic houses in Pomme Valley, these are the ones we think could be hiding the mine. Look at the names. Do you see anything that jumps out at you?"

"Garden!" Dottie breathed, growing excited. "One of the houses is Garden House. Isn't that the one Zachary will be renovating?"

Jillian nodded. "Exactly. We think the mine is hidden inside that house."

Amazed, Dottie glanced over at Sherlock, who had to have the smuggest look I have ever seen on his face. He was panting contentedly, his mouth was open, and he had his long tongue flopped out. Watson was resting—Sphinx-like—on the seat beside him.

"What I don't understand," Jillian continued, as she twisted back around in her seat to face forward, "is how the other pictures fit in. For instance, why is that small yellow car significant? Or the pictures of the book displays in Clara's store?"

I shrugged. "I don't think we're going to know until this case is over, once and for all. That is, unless you know someone who drives a super-small, yellow hatchback?"

"I'm sorry, I don't," Jillian confessed.

"I don't, either," Dottie confirmed.

"What about books?" I continued, as I looked at Dottie in my rearview mirror. "You've seen your mother's store. I mean, it's a bookstore, for crying out loud. Do you have any idea why the dogs would have stopped at those four displays?"

Dottie sadly shook her head. "I don't. I don't even know which four you're talking about. Mom had displays everywhere you look in that little store. Plus, she had all kinds of things on them. Listen, I have a question for you."

"Fire away," I told her, as I navigated around a slow-moving station wagon.

"Since you're investigating my mother's death, I gotta know something." Dottie took a deep breath. "Have you found any leads about my grandfather? I guess what I'm asking is, do you have any idea why he was found on your property? Are there any suspects?"

I sighed and shook my head. "Not yet. Give them some time. I'm sure they can figure it out."

Dottie offered each of the dogs a pat before turning to the window to watch the passing scenery. Ten minutes later, we pulled into the driveway of Garden House. As we all exited the car and the dogs were placed on the ground, we got a closer look at the third oldest house in Pomme Valley.

"It's an eye-sore," I grumbled, as I took in the cracked driveway, broken curbs, and explosive growth of weeds. "I thought it was a PoS then, and now that I see it up close? I think it's a bigger PoS."

The house had definitely seen better days.

The single-story structure sat back from the road by nearly fifty feet. Its windows had long been boarded up, the mailbox was missing, and the post it had been sitting on remained splintered and missing its top third. Siding had been stripped away in places, revealing the framing within the walls. And the roof? Hoo, boy. I'm pretty sure that, whenever it would rain around here, the insides of the house would get thoroughly rinsed.

I was responsible for renovating this place? It'd be easier (and probably cheaper) to simply raze everything to the ground and start over. However, I have this sneaky suspicion that there was going to be no easy way out for me. The city wanted that house restored to its full glory. Well, so be it.

Jillian handed me the key ring as we stepped up to the front door. It was locked? Based on how the door was hanging on its frame, I'll bet I could simply push the door open. Tempting, but no.

Once the door was open, we carefully stepped inside. I say carefully, because there were holes in the floor. Everywhere. Visible through the broken floorboards was dirt, dirt, and more dirt. It also looked as though several animals had been using the house, since I could see some type of animal dung scattered along the exposed ground.

"Let's make sure the dogs don't go anywhere near that," I said, as I turned to look at Jillian. "Looks like we have some type of animal poo over there by the fireplace."

"As long as the animals aren't still in here," Dottie nervously said.

"Agreed," Jillian added, as she wrapped the leash around her hand, thus reducing the slack. "Well, it's not as bad as I had thought."

"No?" I sputtered, as I turned to look at her. "I think it's several times worse, in my opinion. Look up. You can see patches of the sky through the roof."

"A new roof will take care of that," Jillian decided.

"And the floor? There's clearly no foundation."

"Which can be remedied," Jillian said, as she and Watson carefully stepped around a broken patch of wooden floorboards.

We were standing in the living room, which also served as the dining room. The house's heating system sat in the far corner and consisted of one super-rusty, wood-burning stove. As we walked around the room, I could tell the walls had originally been papered, only thanks to whatever had been living in here for the past century or so, most of it had now been reduced to hanging strips. Right on cue, a breeze whipped up outside, which sent the aforementioned strips fluttering in the breeze inside.

I saw an open doorway on my right, which after peering through it, revealed a tiny bedroom. No furniture was present, unless you counted the smashed bits of wood heaped in the far corner. Also, several sections of the floor had been torn away, but I'm assuming humans were to blame, seeing how I could make out the remnants of a hearth. I figured this ramshackle house must have been home to a group of homeless people, and that they were probably just trying to stay warm.

I should also mention I didn't see a bathroom anywhere, let alone see any pipes which would suggest running water. This renovation was going to be an absolute bear to take on. Thankfully, that's what contractors are for.

"Not very homey, is it?" Jillian said, as she steered Watson around yet another broken section of floor.

"Any idea where we're supposed to start looking?" Dottie asked. She stepped around Jillian to stop at the nearest patch of bare earth. "I guess that means the pit mine theory is out."

"I was thinking the same thing," I admitted. "I guess I thought the house was built up and over the mine. This place isn't that big. If this house was sitting over a mine, then I'm pretty sure we'd be able to see it. Besides, there are holes everywhere. Dang. This place couldn't be the right one."

Right then, I felt the leash go taut. Looking down at Sherlock, I saw that the inquisitive corgi was looking at the fireplace. Shrugging, I started heading to the northwestern corner of the house, intent on inspecting the fireplace up close, when Sherlock veered to the right and, instead, led me to the far corner. The floorboards were intact here, which was a nice change. No jump-stepping across any holes, thank you very much. But, no sooner had I turned to check on Jillian when I heard Sherlock let out a low woof.

"What is it?" I asked, as I dropped my voice down low and squatted, so I could drape an arm around the tri-colored corgi. "Do you hear something?"

In response, Sherlock dropped his nose to the ground and sniffed along the base of the wall. He only made it a few feet or so, when he gave a loud snort, and turned around. He sniffed in the opposite direction for about the same distance when he stopped again, made a ninety degree turn to the left, and started over. In this manner, I watched the little corgi outline a four by four foot square. Looking up at me, Sherlock paused, head-tilted, and then sat.

"What's he doing?" Dottie asked.

"He's found something," Jillian excitedly exclaimed. "Zachary, is there something on the ground?"

"Well, there's no animal poo," I reported, as I squatted again. "That's always a plus. Hmm, I don't see anything that stands out. It's nothing but floorboards. Let me try something. Dottie? Would you take Sherlock?"

"Of course."

Squatting low, I ran my hands along the lines Sherlock had sniffed out. It might not have looked any different, but it felt it. Somehow, these boards in the square Sherlock had outlined for me felt rougher; coarser. It was almost as if the surface of the boards were more scuffed up than the rest of the flooring.

I pulled my handy-dandy multi-tool from my belt and unfolded the pliers.

"Do you see something?" Jillian asked, hopefully.

"Possibly. Hold on to that thought. Let's see ... well, well. Would you look at that? This piece is lifting up. Actually, so is this one. And this one. Darned if this doesn't look like a big wooden jigsaw puzzle. Let me clear it out of the way."

Less than two minutes later, with the pieces of the flooring stacked in a neat pile nearby, Sherlock's discovery became apparent to the rest of us: a concealed trapdoor.

"Good job, boy!"

Sherlock's mouth opened and he started panting. Watson approached and nuzzled his side, as if to offer congratulations.

Opening the trapdoor revealed a pitch-black hole, with the upper rungs of a wooden ladder visible.

Jillian handed Watson's leash to Dottie. "I'll be right back. I just so happen to have a flashlight in my car."

"Do you guys do this type of thing all the time?" Dottie asked, as she offered me a grin.

"More than you'd think," I acknowledged, returning the smile. "Whenever these two are concerned, the sky's the limit."

We heard a car door slam shut. Moments later, Jillian passed me a professional-looking Maglite flashlight, the kind which requires four D batteries to run, only this one was purple. I'm sure you've seen the kind. If you were to heft one in your hand, then I'm sure you'd know that you could probably use the thing as a club.

A bright, welcoming swath of light appeared. Once I was assured a bogeyman wasn't waiting for me at the bottom, I handed the flashlight back to Jillian and started down the steps.

"You be careful," Jillian warned. "That ladder looks as though it has seen better days."

"It may look decrepit, but it's very secure," I

assured her, as I tugged on the built-in wooden ladder for emphasis. "All right, I'm down. Can you pass me the light?"

"That's too far for me to reach," Jillian said, shaking her head. "Even if I were to get down on the ground, which, let's face it, is not going to happen, I still wouldn't be able to reach you."

"Drop it down."

"You'll catch it?"

"If I don't, then according to all those commercials I've seen, it should still work."

"I like this flashlight," Jillian said, frowning. "I don't want to break it, and I certainly don't want to scuff it."

"That was a joke, dear. I'll catch it. If, for some reason butterfingers here drops it, then I'll personally buy you a new one."

Jillian's hand sprang open and the flashlight fell. Surprising even myself, I caught it—one-handed—just as it came within reach. I know, right? Not bad for an old man.

"Nice catch, gramps," Dottie snickered.

"Gramps?" I repeated, in a mock-offended tone. "Thanks a lot, Judas."

Laughter trickled down from above me as I spun around to see where I was. Was this it? Were we going to be the ones to locate something people have been searching for since the mid-19th century?

Nope.

I'd like to say I was in a basement, only there

were no windows, no doors (save the trap-door), and no other way out. Root cellar sprang to mind, but if so, what was it doing with its own fireplace? Granted, it was less than a third of the size of the one on the ground floor and, from the looks of things, one was sitting on top of the other. I, for one, didn't know fireplaces could share a chimney, but I guess it made sense. What did it mean? Maybe people had been living down here, too? More likely, I decided, this room was probably used to smoke—and possibly store—meat. Without any windows, and since we were at least a dozen feet below the main level of the house, this storeroom probably stayed really cold.

"What do you see?" Jillian called from above.

"Looks like a storeroom," I said, as I looked up at the open trapdoor.

"I think we have a problem," I heard Dottie's voice say.

Jillian's face turned to look to her left. "What is it? Are the dogs okay?"

"They are not happy about something," Dottie's voice said. "They … look out! Those little sneaks just got away from me! Jillian, watch the door! Watch the door!"

I hurried over so that I was stationed directly under the opening. Just in case. Thankfully, I shouldn't have worried. Both dogs' heads appeared, and both cocked their heads at me, as if they couldn't figure out what I was doing down in a dark, dank hole. After a few moments, Sherlock's head disappeared, but Watson's remained.

"It's okay, guys. There's nothing down here. I'm coming back up."

"Awwooooo!" Sherlock howled from somewhere above.

"Oooooo!" Watson agreed, uttering a low howl. Thankfully, she kept her place.

"Did both of them just howl?" Jillian asked, dumbfounded. "I don't think I've ever heard them do that at the same time."

"That makes two of us," I agreed. "Can you tell why he's howling?"

"Looks like he's directing it at the fireplace," I heard Dottie say.

"Watson? What's the matter? Move out of the way and I'll … no, don't you even think about it. There's no way I could catch you on the ladder. Get that thought out of your little corgi brain."

Both dogs howled again. In unison. I might not have been able to see Sherlock, but I could see Watson. I could say she was howling at me, while whining in anticipation of us being reunited, but that wasn't the case. Besides, it looked as though she was staring through me, at something behind me. Turning, I could see that the little female corgi was howling at the tiny fireplace.

"There's nothing there," I told the dogs. "Would you quit it?"

Neither dog listened to me. Instead, they both howled a third time and Watson tried her best to free herself from Dottie's grip. Thankfully, Dottie was much stronger than she was.

"Oh, no you don't," our new friend said, as she tightened her grip. "You're staying put."

"Zachary? Can you tell what has captured Watson's attention?"

"She's staring at the fireplace."

"She couldn't be," I heard Jillian's voice say. "Unless you're telling me there's a fireplace down in the cellar, too?"

"There is," I confirmed. "A tiny one. If I were to venture a guess, then I'd say it was used for smoking meat."

"Sherlock is howling at this one," I heard Dottie say, "and Watson is howling at the one down there. What does it mean?"

"I'm coming back up," I decided. "Hang on."

Once I had rejoined my companions, I turned to see for myself why Sherlock had become fascinated with the fireplace. And, for the record, I could not. But, the moment I rejoined the pack, as the corgis would've put it, Watson lost interest in the trapdoor and immediately joined Sherlock. Together, they both stared at the fireplace and howled again.

"What is with you two?" I wanted to know, as I headed for the gray limestone fireplace. "Happy? I'm here. Now, what's up?"

The corgis fell silent as they gazed up at the large stone fireplace. Both slowly lowered themselves into a *down* position and appeared to make themselves comfortable, as if neither planned on moving for the next couple of hours. Sighing heavily, I approached the stone hearth and ran my fingers along the gray limestone. No, there were no hidden switches or concealed doors. It was just as it appeared: a fireplace.

Just as I stepped away, intent on retrieving the dogs' leashes, I hesitated. Something I had just seen didn't make sense. I curiously approached the fireplace a second time and leaned forward for a better look.

"What is it?" Jillian asked.

I reached out and traced my finger around a small, half-inch hole under the left lip of the mantel. "I thought this might have originally been from a missing gas pipe, as the hole is the right size for a residential gas line, only I'm pretty sure that, based on the age of the house, this fireplace only burned wood. Or, perhaps, coal, I guess. Either way, I know it's not gas so the question remains: what is this?"

Jillian crowded close and inspected the area for herself. "Well, it is a hole. I can think of several plausible explanations. The stone here could have chipped. The mortar might have broken off and fallen away. Or, maybe the rock always looked that way? You never know. It might just be a natural occurrence."

"Which one are you talking about?" Dottie wanted to know. "The lower one or the upper one?"

Jillian and I abandoned the first hole and

looked up at Dottie, who was standing over us and looking at a spot on the top of the mantel, just a few inches away.

"Two holes?" Jillian curiously asked. "Are there any others?"

A quick search of the fireplace revealed it only had the two. I was about ready to say it had to be a fluke when I caught sight of the dogs. Both were staring straight at the fireplace, and darned if it didn't look like they were watching us inspect the holes.

"This top one is definitely smaller," Jillian reported. "And it looks as though the hole is man-made."

"The key," I quietly murmured to myself.

Jillian looked up. "What was that? Zachary, did you say something?"

"The key," I repeated, growing excited once more. "Do you remember what Derrick Halloway said? Back at the nursing home? The last thing Charlie Hanson told him was that he had found the key."

"He also said that no one has ever found any traces of that key," Jillian reminded me. "Mr. Halloway searched for ten years and didn't find anything."

I turned back to the holes and studied them for a few moments longer. If I was right, then that piece would fit there, while allowing that part to go there. So, that was why it appeared broken!

I felt a nudge on my shoulder. Jillian was there

and was smiling at me. She tapped the side of my head.

"Hey, would you let us in on what's going on in there? I can see you've worked something out. What is it?"

"I believe," I began, as I tapped the two holes, "that these are key holes. And the only way to find out what's waiting for us would be to use the key!"

"What key?" Jillian wanted to know. "I haven't seen any key."

"Neither have I," Dottie added.

"Yes, you have," I argued, as I looked at our new friend. "Charlie was right. He had located the key. You used to play with it all the time."

Jillian's face lit up. "Oooo, I think I know where you're going with this!"

"Would someone care to clue me in?" Dottie complained.

"Your pirate sword," I said, as I headed for the door. "I think it just might be in the back of the car. Give me just a moment."

I hurried out to Jillian's SUV, opened the back door, and smiled as I saw the Sticking Tommy right where I'd left it. Carefully picking it up, I hurried back inside. Dottie's eyes widened as I strode back to the fireplace.

"That?" Clara's daughter sputtered. "You think that is the key? It can't be. It's been broken for a number of years now."

I held up the wicked spike-looking thing and

tapped the part with the hook shape on it. "You've always believed that this part is broken. That it's not supposed to slide up and down like this."

Dottie nodded. "That's right. I think I just played with it one too many times."

"I think it was made like that on purpose," I argued. "Usually, these things are driven into the rock, or wherever the miner is working, and a candle is placed in this holder next to the hook."

"Then, what is the hook for?" Dottie asked. "If you drive the spike into the wall, or ground, or wherever, why do you need that hook?"

"It was probably used to hang on something," Jillian theorized. "If you were unable to drive the spike into the wall, then you'd have the ability to simply hang it on something, like an overhead beam."

I nodded. "Exactly."

"But it's broken!" Dottie insisted.

"Is it?" I asked. "If I'm right about this, then this hook goes here," I said, as I placed the tip of the hook into the smaller top hole, "and then that means the spike part of it goes into the lower hole. See? Everything lines up!"

"If the hook part wasn't broken," Dottie slowly began, "then you wouldn't be able to insert the spike into the hole, is that it?"

I shook my head. "Umm, not exactly. Look. Do you see the way it's hooked to the fireplace? I haven't moved anything, and it still lines up perfectly. Red Dawg ingeniously took a commonly used tool, made a few modifications, and turned it into the only way to access his precious mine. Without this, you'd only find an empty house."

"Candles!" Jillian groaned. She held out a hand. "Zachary, could I see your phone?"

I shrugged. "Sure. What's the matter?"

Jillian opened my recently taken photos and shook her head with amazement. She looked down at Sherlock and Watson, who were both lounging on the floor, and gave them each a pat on the head. She then leaned forward to tap the round candle holder.

"That's why the dogs have shown so much interest in candles. This Sticking Tommy thing-amajig is nothing more than a candle holder! Do you see these pictures? In each and every one of the pictures taken inside A Lazy Afternoon, the common denominator in the photos are candles! Look!"

As I scrolled through the pictures, I nodded. Sure enough, I could see candles in each of the four displays the dogs had expressed an interest in. That couldn't be a coincidence.

"With the candle holder part not attached to the spike," Dottie slowly reasoned, "that would mean you..."

"That's right," I confirmed, after Dottie trailed off. "I believe that once the spike is inserted, the mine will be unlocked, and we can finally prove Red Dawg's lost gold mine has been found."

Turning, I gripped the large handle of the spike

and prepared to push. However, both dogs started growling and barking before I could thrust the spike into the hole. Then I heard the unmistakable sound of a gun being cocked.

"That's far enough, Mr. Anderson," a cold, very familiar voice sneered.

Turning, the three of us came face-to-face with a person with a gun aimed at us. It was a woman, one with whom I was very familiar: Abigail Lawson.

TWELVE

O h, you've got to be kidding me," I groaned, as I took in the smug expression on Abigail's face. "What on earth are you doing here? Trying to get the drop on us?"

"I already have, Mr. Anderson."

"Abigail," Jillian hesitantly began, "I realize the two of us don't really know each other, but don't you think this is the wrong thing to do?"

"Shut up!" Abigail snarled, as she tightened her grip on the revolver.

"I knew it," I muttered, as I stared at the business end of Abigail's gun. "You are responsible for all of it, aren't you? Charlie Hanson's murder and now his daughter, Clara. What kind of a sick nutjob are you?"

"I did not kill Charlie Hanson!" Abigail cried. The gun wavered in her hand, as though it was becoming too difficult to hold. "I was ten years old when Charlie disappeared. Ten! Do you think I could have killed him as a child?"

I didn't have to think about the answer. "Easily."

Jillian shook her head. "Agreed."

"You've convinced me," Dottie sarcastically added, as she eyed the gun in Abigail's hands.

"Believe me, don't believe me, I don't care," Abigail said, as her nose lifted. After a few moments, she turned to look at me and there was no chance of missing the look that swept across her features. "I hate you, Mr. Anderson. I've hated you ever since I learned Mother gave away her estate. That winery was mine! Mine, do you hear?"

"Abigail," I said, as softly and gently as I could, "if you truly believe that, then you did not know your own mother nearly as well as you think. I've read the letters. I've seen the photo albums. There was no way she was going to let her life's work be sold off to the highest bidder. I'm even inclined to believe that she wanted you to take over the winery, only once she learned what you really wanted, she made sure that would never happen."

"And what is it you think I *really* want?" Abigail sneered.

"Money," I answered. "Money, money, and then more money. Haven't you figured it out yet? If you would have expressed a desire to keep the winery in the family, then we wouldn't be having this conversation. I would probably be living in Phoenix, and you would have yourself your own winery. But, since you have stated over and over about how you wanted to sell to a big-name corporation, then your mother knew she had to find someone else to take over Lentari Cellars. Want to blame someone for this whole mess? Well, blame yourself."

Yeah, I can admit it now. That probably wasn't my best move ever. What can I say? I have a knack for pushing people's buttons.

"You dare accuse me of creating this mess?" Abigail practically screeched. "If it wasn't for you, my daughter wouldn't be in jail. If you had never moved here, Lentari Cellars would have been mine! If not for you, I wouldn't be driving around in a God-forsaken compact car!"

My eyebrows lifted. Abigail was currently driving a compact car? I thought back to the pictures I had taken in order to mollify Sherlock and Watson, and remembered the tiny yellow sub-compact car. No … the dogs weren't that good, were they?

"You're driving a compact car? It wouldn't be a small yellow Toyota, would it?"

For the first time that I could remember, Abigail was speechless.

"You couldn't possibly have known," Abigail whispered. "No one knew I had that blasted car. I made sure of it."

Let me pause here a moment and ask a question: have you ever had a case of the giggles and couldn't compose yourself? No matter how hard you tried, no matter what disgusting thought you could think of, nothing could break the cycle of giggles? Well, I made the mistake of picturing Ms. Cranky Pants behind the wheel of her no-bigger-than-a-wheelbarrow car and started chuckling. I risked a glance at Jillian. To say she wasn't pleased with me would be an understatement.

"What are you laughing for?" she hissed at me. "She has a gun! Compose yourself!"

"I'm trying," I squeezed out, between laughs. "You heard her. She was the one driving that little yellow car. That's why the dogs were interested in those passing cars. She must have been driving by."

"I'd listen to her," Abigail coldly advised me. "Not only can I hear you, but as your significant other pointed out, I do have a gun. You'd do well to remember that."

I finally managed to get control of my laughing. But, no matter how hard I tried, I couldn't wipe the grin from my face. Little old Abigail in the teeny, tiny car. Oh, that was priceless!

I had to change the subject quickly or else I was going to start laughing again.

"You say you aren't responsible for Charlie's murder," I slowly began, "but you don't deny killing Clara. Why would you do it? What has she ever done to you?"

"I didn't want to kill her," Abigail admitted, reluctantly, "but I didn't have a choice. She wouldn't give me the key. She wouldn't even admit that she had it."

"That's because she didn't know that she did," I returned. I pointed at the antique piece of mining equipment still dangling from the mantel. "Does that look like a key to you?"

"That's the key?" Abigail repeated, as she stared at the strange-looking device. "You're lying."

"Now you know why Clara said she didn't have the key you were looking for," Jillian stated, as she frowned. "How did you even know she had the key?"

"I knew she had it," Abigail snapped. "Who else would have had it? My father never talked about that gold mine, but I knew he was looking for it. The only thing he'd tell me was that fame and fortune were waiting for him, just around the corner."

"He thought his ship was about to come in, too, huh?" I muttered, shaking my head. "Been talking to Derrick Halloway, haven't you?"

"I know you paid him a visit," Abigail said, nodding. "Well, so did I. I had to know what the two of you had been talking about."

"He told you about the key," Jillian guessed.

"Of course. Why wouldn't he? He knew who my parents were."

"Then, he'd have to know how much of a whack-a-doodle you really are," I flatly stated, as I started to cross my arms over my chest. Both Sherlock and Watson started to growl and, if possible, inched closer to Abigail.

"Spewing insults isn't going to change today's outcome," Abigail snidely informed me.

Right then, I was reminded of a few days ago, when I was sitting in an interrogation room at PVPD's headquarters. Looking at the woman before me, I realized right then just how I ended up on the police's hot seat again.

"You talked to Taylor."

Jillian and Dottie both turned to look at me, as if they weren't too sure what I was doing.

"The tire iron," I continued. "You used it to kill Clara Hanson, remember? Well, no wonder it had my prints on it. That was because it really was my tire iron. Taylor must've stolen it when she was down in Phoenix, stalking me."

"I thought, at first, she wasn't going to talk to me," Abigail admitted. "She said she preferred to simply rot away in some prison cell, but once I told her why I was there, well, her tune certainly changed. As soon as my daughter found out that she could help put you away once and for all, well, she begged me to take it. She said your prints were still on that thing, and that it'd make a great murder weapon. I had to agree."

"And just like that?" I said, as I glared at Abigail. "You decide to kill Clara and try to pin it on me?"

Abigail shrugged. "It was a worth a shot. I tried, it didn't work, no loss."

"No loss?" Dottie angrily repeated. "That's my mother you're talking about!"

"And she had something that didn't belong to her!" Abigail shouted back.

"Oh, yeah?" I shot back. "And what would

that be? Possessing the key to Red Dawg's lost gold mine? It once belonged to Charlie Hanson. By right, it passed to Clara, his daughter. If that doesn't make it hers, then I don't know what will."

"That key should never have fallen into that witless woman's hands," Abigail snapped.

"And whose hands do you think it should have gone to?" I asked. "Yours?"

"Who else? My family's, of course."

"Yeah, right," I scoffed. "I'd love to hear you explain that messed up logic."

Abigail fell silent. Jillian, on the other hand, looked at the older woman and her eyes widened. "You know something about Charlie Hanson's death, don't you? If it wasn't you, and I'm inclined to believe a young girl would be incapable of cold-blooded murder, then who was it?"

"It couldn't possibly be Bonnie," I whispered, as I realized Jillian was right. Abigail was protecting someone. "Your mother had her hands full taking care of the winery. Another family member, perhaps?"

"I'll bet her father did it," Dottie quietly muttered.

Then it clicked. Abigail's father! He must have grown tired of waiting for his ship to come in, and seeing how Charles Hanson's had just arrived, became jealous.

"When did you figure out your father was responsible for Charlie Hanson's murder?"

"I eavesdropped on him and some other man

one night, not long after the blood was discovered and Charlie Hanson was reported missing," Abigail quietly recalled. "I didn't know the identity of the other man, nor did I really care. It wasn't important. What was important was what I heard. My dad, confiding to his friend what he had done. He said he had broken into the Hanson house. He had turned the place upside down, looking for this key, whatever it was. When he couldn't find it, he grew so angry that, when Charlie came home, he flew into a rage. He went at Charlie with a crowbar, demanding he tell him where this key had been hidden."

"Charlie never told," I guessed.

Abigail nodded. "It enraged my father even more. I heard my father say he was horrified at what he had done to Charlie. He knew he had committed murder, and was scared. So, he took the body out to the far corner of the property, but could not bring himself to bury him on his land."

"That's why he chose the Parson's land," Jillian said.

"How did he manage to get Charlie under that rock?" I asked. "That's what I want to know. You didn't see the size of that boulder I had to bust apart. It was huge."

"I can only assume my father was afraid the body would be discovered when the land was tilled and farmed, so he buried the body deep. He must have figured stashing the body under a huge boulder would be a safe hiding place."

"And now, you have killed Clara," I added. "For the exact same reason: greed. Poor Clara did have the key, but she didn't know it. For the record, we found that thing buried in her basement."

Abigail scowled. "I searched the basement. It was not there. You're lying again."

"I never lied the first time," I said. "And I didn't say it was at her house. That thing? The key? It was at Dottie's store. We found a small basement at the bookstore. There were a lot of antiques down there."

"Blacksmithing tools," Jillian recalled.

"Right," I said, nodding. "That key was in a box full of blacksmithing tools. Don't you get it? It was hiding in plain sight. That miner's candleholder, well, it looks a lot like a blacksmithing tool. Charlie probably thought it'd be safe there."

"You killed my mother," Dottie accused, as she looked at Abigail. "How can you live with yourself?"

"Very easily," Abigail admitted, with a smirk.

"You took my mother from me!" Dottie screamed, as she lunged forward.

Thankfully, I reached her before Abigail could react.

"Now's not the time," I told the girl, who had started sobbing hysterically.

"I'll never be able to talk to her again!" Dottie continued, in a shaky voice. "I'll never be able to reconcile! I won't ever be able to tell her how sorry I was for how I behaved. You took that from me!"

The gun finally swung around, aimed toward Dottie.

"She'll be fine," I assured Abigail, as I stepped between her and Dottie. "No more problems."

"Be sure of it," Abigail snarled. "If she opens her mouth again, then three generations of Hansons will have suffered the same disastrous fate. Do you understand me?"

Jillian nodded. "We do." She took Dottie's hand and forcefully pulled her away from me and Abigail.

"All that trouble, to keep the key out of my family's hands," Abigail chuckled. The gun she was holding swung around until it was aimed back on me. "You. Pass it to me."

Eyeing Jillian, I shrugged. I passed the dogs' leashes over to her and then reached over to unhook the Sticking Tommy from the mantel. Without saying a word, the strange contraption was passed to Abigail, who took the long metal spike and gave it a condescending look.

"You're telling me this is the key?"

I nodded. "Yep. And, I will tell you that I'm pretty sure the mine is located right here, in this house."

Abigail smirked. "I thought as much. Now, where is it?"

"Zachary, what are you doing?" Jillian hissed at me. "What did you tell her that for?"

I patted her hand and turned back to Abigail.

"I can tell you, but there's something you should know first."

"And what's that?" Abigail all but growled.

"That you won't be allowed to keep anything you find in this house."

"Of course I will," Abigail contradicted. "All I have to do is simply purchase this house with the gold waiting to be discovered, and then everything will be legal."

"This is a registered historic house," I reminded her. "You might find that difficult, especially since it isn't for sale."

"Everything is for sale," Abigail argued. "All you have to do is find the right price."

"Trust me on this one," I argued back. "This house isn't for sale, nor will it ever be for the foreseeable future."

Abigail's eyes narrowed. "You have no way of knowing that."

I looked at the gun Abigail had trained on me and smiled. "I say that because, and I'm sorry to say that you aren't gonna like this, I own this house. I just bought it, actually."

The color drained out of Abigail's face. "You're lying."

"You're too late," I insisted. "Garden House is mine. And, since both of us believe Red Dawg's mine is going to be found somewhere inside this house, that makes the mine, well, mine."

"I don't believe you."

"Believe it," Dottie said, raising her voice. "I

was listening as these two talked to the mayor. Zachary bought this house, and Jillian purchased two others, which could've been the hiding place of the mine."

Abigail stubbornly shook her head. "No."

"It is true," Jillian added. "Please believe us."

Abigail sighed, as if she had just made up her mind about something. Hopefully, it didn't involve the gun.

"No matter. You'll just sign this house over to me."

"You think I'm gonna sign something else over to you?" I scoffed. "How well do you think that's going to work for you?"

Abigail hefted her gun and gave me a malicious grin. "I'm thinking I will finally be able to persuade you, once and for all."

"That's never going to work," I pointed out. "There's too much paperwork involved. I mean, you've gotta fill out applications, get documents notarized, and so on. How do you think that'll look to a notary public if there's a gun pointed at my face?"

"Then, I'll just have to point it somewhere more productive."

"Such as?" I challenged.

The gun was then pointed at Jillian. Oh, snap. Challenge accepted.

"Listen," I began, as I held up my hands. "Don't do anything stupid."

"I know you're a widow," Abigail began, as she

addressed Jillian, "and I know you're engaged. To him. You will tell Mr. Anderson to sign over this house, or so help me, I will pull this trigger."

Whether it was the seriousness of the situation, or the simple fact that I was tired of dealing with Abigail Lawson, one thing became crystal clear: I couldn't give a rat's about that stupid mine. If Abigail wanted it badly enough to put Jillian in harm's way, then I wanted nothing more to do with it.

"Look," I angrily said, drawing Abigail's attention, "if you want this house so bad, I'll tell you what. You can have it."

"What?" Dottie sputtered.

"There are provisions," I added, as I glared at Abigail. "Are you willing to listen?"

"I'm the one with the gun," Abigail flatly pointed out. "I'll be making the provisions, thank you very much."

"No," I argued, "you won't. Hear me out. If you want this house so freakin' bad, then you can have it. The provisions are, I want you out of our lives. Forever. I don't ever want to see you again."

"Zachary…" Jillian began.

Both dogs started barking.

"Nope," I interrupted, cutting Jillian off. "That's the deal. You, Abigail Lawson, will sever all ties with Pomme Valley and you will clear out. Agree to that, and this house will be yours."

"Umm, it's a historic house," Jillian quietly reminded me. "We promised we wouldn't sell."

My eyes widened. "Oh. Dang, that's right. Okay, then here's what we do. I won't touch this house until you're done taking whatever you want from the mine. Do we have a deal?"

Abigail stared at me for a few moments before finally nodding. Then, she turned to Jillian and pulled out her phone.

"You. Start recording. I'm going to do the same."

Jillian hurriedly pulled out her phone.

"Now," Abigail began, as she turned to face me, and held up her phone to make a recording, "repeat what you just told me."

I did, word for word.

"Am I stealing anything from this house?"

"You have my complete permission to take whatever you want from this house. I will give you, what, three months to do it? Will that be enough time?"

Abigail nodded. "It should. And then? I will be more than happy to agree to your request and leave this pathetic little town once and for all."

"Then we have a deal," I said, as I faced Abigail's phone, and then Jillian. "Satisfied?"

Abigail nodded. "Yes. You said this is the key? Where's the mine?"

I pointed at the fireplace. "I'm pretty sure it's through there."

"How?"

"Come here. No, knock it off. I'm not going to do anything. I gave you my word. Honor yours by putting that gun away."

For the first time, Abigail finally nodded, lowered her gun, and shoved it back into her purse, but not before I caught a glimpse of the handle.

"Is your gun pink?" I sniggered.

Abigail bristled with annoyance. "What of it?"

"Nothing, I guess. I didn't know they made pink revolvers. Whatever. Now, stand here. Do you see this hole?"

"Yes. What about it?"

"Abigail, that's the keyhole. You aren't tall enough to see the top of the mantel, so put your hand here, where mine is. Feel the second hole?"

"Yes."

"Good. Now, put the hook in the top hole, and then turn the spike part until it lines up with the lower hole. See how it lines up?"

"I do. Now what?"

"That's as far as we got. I'm assuming you push."

At that exact moment, as Abigail braced herself to shove the spiky, pointed part of the Sticking Tommy into the keyhole, both Sherlock and Watson freaked the ever-lovin' eff out. Both of the dogs pulled themselves free from Jillian's grip and bolted for the door. Abigail, too intent on gaining access to the mine, either didn't see or didn't care. However, I have learned to follow the dogs' instincts at all times.

Grabbing Jillian's hand with my right, and Dottie's with my left, the three of us hauled butt out of the room just as Abigail gave the spike a solid shove. The last thing I heard, as we cleared the door, was a loud grating sound, followed by a very audible hissing noise.

I had just reclaimed the leashes outside, on the porch, when I caught the first whiff of the rotten egg stench.

"That's hydrogen sulfide!" Jillian cried. "Get back! Get far back! That gas is highly poisonous!"

The three of us, plus the two dogs, ran nearly twenty yards down the driveway before I turned to look back at the house. Even from this distance, I could smell the fumes of that noxious gas.

"Abigail," I breathed.

Yes, she was a despicable human being but, no, she didn't deserve to die like that. No one did. I was about to pull my shirt up over my nose and run back inside when I felt two sets of arms grab me tight.

"Don't even think about it," Jillian warned me. "It's way too dangerous."

"You're not going back in there," Dottie added.

"What about Abigail?" I protested.

"I'm sorry, Zachary," Jillian said. "There's no way anyone could survive that much gas. Even if Abigail is somehow still alive, I won't risk you going back inside that house."

E xactly one week later, Jillian and I were quietly sitting in the back of City Hall, listening to the town council go over new laws, restrictions, and increases in various fees. Looking around the room, I could see that nearly every seat had been filled. And why shouldn't they be? It had been announced in the newspaper that Red Dawg's lost gold mine had been located, and it was confirmed to be in Pomme Valley. Everyone wanted to know where it was and, undoubtedly, wanted to know if they were—somehow—going to walk away with a piece of it.

"That mine killed someone," I heard one voice whisper, close by.

"You heard no such thing," another argued.

"Did so. Opened it up and whoosh! Poisonous gas spilled out."

"Do we know who was killed? Do you think it was a booby trap?"

"Well, duh! Ol' Red Dawg himself must still be

guardin' it."

"You're a dork."

"Bite me."

On and on it went. I looked over at Jillian, clutched her hand tightly, and gave her an encouraging smile.

"I can see why the mayor wanted to address this," I whispered. "I have a feeling the stories will only get more and more elaborate."

"And far-fetched," Jillian agreed.

The group of four men and women seated at the front of the room, behind their large, wooden counter, suddenly stood and raised their arms to get everyone's attention.

"Ladies and gentlemen," one of the guys began, "may I have your..."

The councilman trailed off as he realized not a single person was paying attention to him. He rectified the matter by banging the gavel in front of him a few times. Once everyone had settled, and the other three council members had taken their seats, the lead councilman tried again.

"Ladies and gentlemen. Due to recent events, the city of Pomme Valley has convened this special session to address your concerns. We have decided..."

"Has it been found?" a deep voice boomed out.

"Mr. Johnson, please take your seat," the councilman pleaded.

Burt Johnson was the owner of Hidden Relic Antiques, and was single-handedly the biggest guy

I have ever seen. Tall, ripped, and as intimidating as anything. But, I will also say that he has to be one of the friendliest people I have ever met, provided you could overlook the fact that he could probably pound you into the ground like a railroad spike if you ever angered him.

"I will, if you answer the question," Burt good-naturedly responded.

Affirmative grunts could be heard coming from all four corners of the meeting hall.

"I will, indeed, Mr. Johnson," the councilman insisted. "Now, before I reveal the location of the mine, I need to remind you people that a police car has been stationed in front of the house, and a private security firm has already been hired. They'll be here later in the day to take over security."

"The mine has truly been found," someone said.

"It has," the councilman confirmed. "And I'll also remind each and every one of you to be on your best behavior. Do not try to enter this mine yourself. I know the desire may be great, but it's simply too dangerous."

"Did someone die in there?" a male voice shouted out.

I recognized Spencer 'Woody' Woodson, owner of Toy Closet. He and his daughter, Zoe, were sitting a couple of rows away. True to her age, Zoe had her phone and was completely oblivious to the outside world.

"There was a fatality," the councilman confirmed. "Hydrogen sulfide gas, a common side effect for poorly circulated mines, had built up and, once the mine was opened, came pouring out. The person who opened the mine didn't have a chance, I'm afraid."

"Who was it?" a woman's voice asked.

"A former PV resident, Ms. Abigail Lawson."

A collective round of gasps and exclamations echoed around the room.

The councilman began patting the air. "People, please. Calm yourselves. I realize many of you knew Ms. Lawson..."

"I knew she was a pain in the --" a male voice darkly muttered.

Several people snorted with amusement. The councilman was one of them. His face understandably reddened, and he hastily cleared his throat.

"The mine has been deemed off limits to everyone, including the owner of the house."

"Whose house?"

"The house currently belongs to Zack Anderson."

I sighed as the grumbling and muttering began.

"That dude was born with a silver spoon in his mouth," one man complained.

"Given his own winery, free and clear, and now this? He owns a gold mine? That ain't fair, man."

The grumblings grew in volume until a middle-aged woman, sitting off to the side of the four council members, rose to her feet. The instant she stood, the hall fell deathly quiet.

"Mayor Campbell," the councilman acknowledged. "Would you care to say a few words?"

The mayor nodded. "I would. People of Pomme Valley, there are a few things you must know. Ms. Lawson has, indeed, passed away. She…"

"He needs to be arrested!" a shrill voice shouted.

"Who speaks?" Mayor Campbell asked, as she looked around the room. "Come, come, after an outburst like that? Surely, you don't want to hide now."

A thin, gray-haired man cautiously rose to his feet. The mayor's smile thinned noticeably.

"Ah, Mr. Peabody. Thank you for attending tonight's session. Do you have something you'd like to get off your chest?"

"That sumbitch needs to be arrested for what he done to Abby."

"I assume you're referring to Ms. Lawson," Mayor Campbell smoothly said, "and what *someone* did. Also, you will refrain from swearing in here. We are conducting official business, is that clear?"

Mr. Peabody's head fell. "Yes, ma'am."

"Excellent. Now, who is the someone you are talking about? Who should be arrested on Ms. Lawson's account?"

Mr. Peabody swung his thin arm out and rotated until he was pointing straight at me.

"Him. The wine dude. He's the one who murdered Abigail."

"That's Henry Peabody," Jillian whispered in my ear. "He's the owner of Pomme Valley Mercantile."

"The hardware store?" I sputtered, as I glared at the angry old man who was defiantly glaring back at me. "So, this is who tipped off Abigail that we were in the store?"

Jillian nodded.

"Mr. Anderson didn't kill Abigail Lawson," the mayor was saying. "The mine has that distinction, as I've already explained."

"Well," Mr. Peabody snapped, after a moment's pause, "then he should be arrested for..."

"That will be enough," Mayor Campbell smoothly cut in.

I had to hand it to the mayor. She hadn't raised her voice one bit, but based on Henry Peabody's posture you would have thought she had just screamed at him for hours on end. Mr. Peabody hastily sat.

"Now, I came up here to quell the disapproving looks, the mutterings under the breath, and so on. Now, you all now know Mr. Anderson owns the house where the mine was found. As a matter of fact, he, and his lovely fiancée, have purchased several homes here in town, with the intent of restoring them to their full glory."

"So you say," Henry Peabody grumbled.

"And we're done with you," Mayor Campbell coolly replied. "Chief Nelson? Would you care to do the honors?"

The Pomme Valley chief of police, who happened to be sitting in the front row, made eye contact with several of his officers and then jerked his head in the direction of the exit. Once the surly business owner had been removed, the mayor continued.

"I've already spoken with Mr. Anderson about the matter," the mayor was saying. "He is a man of his word. Once the house has been renovated, and after the infamous Red Dawg Gold Mine has been deemed safe, the house, property, and mine will be given back to the city."

Every single whispered conversation in the City Hall was silenced. Heads began turning my way.

"Pomme Valley's favorite wine maker is not interested in profiting from the mine," the mayor assured the crowd.

"Bull," one voice disagreed.

"It's true," I admitted, standing up. Jillian quickly rose to her feet beside me. "I couldn't give a fig about that mine. Believe me, don't believe me, it doesn't matter."

"What about Charlie Hanson?" another voice shouted.

"Yeah, tell us about ol' Charlie! Who did him in?"

"I'll bet Abigail did it," a third voice said.

"What about poor Clara? Who killed her?" yet another voice demanded.

"That's enough, people," Mayor Campbell said, as her gaze swept across the room. "Detective Samuelson, would you care to fill everyone in?"

My friend Vance, sitting on the other side of me, calmly rose. He pulled out his notebook, flipped it open, and began to read.

"Charles S. Hanson, resident of Pomme Valley. Disappeared in the summer of 1968, only to re-appear just last week. His remains were uncovered at Lentari Cellars, on land recently purchased from the Parson family. He..."

"Just tell us who's responsible for the murders!" the voice insisted.

Vance shrugged. "Hank Davies was responsible for Charles Hanson's murder. Hank learned Charlie Hanson was days away from locating the mine and, I'm sorry to say, was too tempted to pass up the opportunity to make some fast cash."

"Isn't he..." one woman began.

"Yes," Vance interrupted. "He's Abigail Lawson's father."

"Where is he now?" someone demanded.

"Hank Davies has been dead for over thirty years," Vance reported. "As for Charlie's daughter, namely Ms. Clara Hanson, well, I'm sorry to say she was murdered by the aforementioned Abigail Lawson. Ms. Lawson believed Clara Hanson held the key to locating the mine. As such, all charges have been dropped against Mr. Zachary Anderson. Are there any other questions?"

"Where is the mine?" one woman demanded.

"That's all I want to know."

"I'm not authorized to answer that," Vance said, as he sat down.

"Thank you, Detective Samuelson," Mayor Campbell said, as she adjusted the microphone on the podium. "Keep the Davies family and the Hanson family in your prayers, please. I'd also like to take a moment and welcome Darla Hanson, Clara's daughter. She will be taking over ownership of A Lazy Afternoon. I expect you all to offer her a warm welcome. Ms. Hanson, would you stand for a moment?"

Dottie, sitting on the other side of Jillian, slowly rose to her feet. She offered the mayor a smile and a shy wave before hurriedly reclaiming her seat.

"If that's all the new business, then we can move on to..."

"All I wanna know is which house has been hiding Red Dawg's mine," one man interrupted, springing to his feet. "If Mr. Anderson is the owner, then I suppose it wouldn't take much to figure it out, would it?"

"Yeah!" another agreed.

Mayor Campbell took a deep breath and readied her answer, only before she could respond Chief Nelson hastily rose to his feet.

"Ma'am? If you'll allow me? Chester, back in your seat. Now, would it be possible to figure out which house has the mine? Probably. However, the last thing I need right now is to wonder if some bonehead is going to try to sneak in when it isn't safe. I've already spoken with this private security company Mr. Anderson has hired, which will be guarding the mine. They know to stop anyone, and I do mean *anyone*, from entering the premises. I'm going to say this now: if you manage to figure out where the mine is, and are caught trespassing, you will be prosecuted to the fullest extent of the law. Do I make myself clear? Only when that mine has been thoroughly examined, and the threat to society removed, will I allow anyone near it. People, do we understand each other?" When no one spoke, the chief nodded, and sat.

The impromptu session ended, and the crowd of people dispersed. Our car was silent as we drove back to my house, each of us being lost in our own thoughts. The last thing I personally wanted was for the good people of PV to despise me any more than they already did. I'm also very glad that Chief Nelson decided not to disclose the mine's location. And, do you know what? It made perfect sense. Gold had a tendency to entice good people to make bad decisions.

"We're back," Jillian announced, as she opened the front door and stepped through.

Sherlock and Watson immediately jumped down from the couch they had been sleeping on and gave themselves a thorough shaking. Squatting low, I gave each of the dogs an ear-rubbing, which had the effect of making them close their eyes and grunt with satisfaction.

As Jillian and I gratefully sank down onto the couch, and the dogs jumped up to lay on either side of us, I heard a fluttering of wings. I tapped my shoulder and waited for the winery's newest resident to appear. Two small claws were suddenly gripping my shoulder and then I felt the little gray parrot nuzzle the side of my face.

"Hey there, Ruby. It's good to see you, too. Don't worry. We'll take good care of you. Your mother would have liked that."

I looked down and caught both dogs looking up at the parrot. Sherlock tilted his head as he stared at Ruby, and I could only hope he wasn't wondering what I think he was wondering: is this thing original or extra crispy?

AUTHOR'S NOTE

Here's hoping you enjoyed the story. I've been having a lot of fun with Zack and the gang. Plus, it's always interesting to keep things progressing in PV. I have to ask myself, now that some time has passed, what's changed? What would I expect to see? Businesses, relationships, and even new people showing up in town are just a part of life, so I try to make it as realistic as possible.

Yes, I did kill off two characters in this book. Clara I've known about for quite some time. I always intended to have her estranged daughter return to her hometown to carry on in her mother's footsteps, but in her own way. As for Abigail, well, who among you didn't want to see that happen? I don't think there was anyone out there who would argue that it shouldn't have happened to her. When I started CCF10, I had no plans to kill off Abigail, but as I started thinking about what I knew of mines, and especially if an older mine had sat — unmolested — for decades and decades, then the last thing you want to do is open it, unprepared. So, the ending essentially wrote itself, and just like that, no more annoying-as-hell Abigail. But, don't count that family out just yet. If ever a family had a reason to hate Zack, it'd certainly be that one. I should also point out that it's a big family. Lots of family members.

Well, what now? I can tell you that I'll be putting PV on hold for just a little bit. That new fantasy series of mine, Dragons of Andela, needs a little TLC, so it's time to get that one finished. Then, as you might have noticed, the gang will be back in a holiday-themed story, *Case of the Great Cranberry Caper*. Someone has decided to steal all the cranberries in Pomme Valley, and no one knows why.

That's it for now. Andela is calling. Gotta see what Jerica

and her reptilian friend have been up to. This is also the part where I ask ... if you enjoyed the book, please consider leaving a review at your favorite retailer. The more the reviews, the better people can find the book!

Happy reading!

J.

July, 2020

What's next for Zack and the corgis?
Case of the Great Cranberry Caper
Zack, Jillian, and the corgis find themselves in the midst
of a new mystery with a Thanksgiving twist. Just as they
are planning a big holiday dinner, someone is breaking
into stores and stealing only the cranberries! Will the
corgi duo, Sherlock and Watson, be able to sniff out
the clues and discover who is behind the treacherous
deed, in time to save holiday meals everywhere?

The Corgi Case Files Series
Available in e-book and paperback

Case of the One-Eyed Tiger
Case of the Fleet-Footed Mummy
Case of the Holiday Hijinks
Case of the Pilfered Pooches
Case of the Muffin Murders
Case of the Chatty Roadrunner
Case of the Highland House Haunting
Case of the Ostentatious Otters
Case of the Dysfunctional Daredevils
Case of the Abandoned Bones
Case of the Great Cranberry Caper

If you enjoy Epic Fantasy, check out Jeff's other series:
Pirates of Perz
Tales of Lentari
Bakkian Chronicles

Sign up for Jeffrey's newsletter to get all the latest
corgi news—
Click here

Manufactured by Amazon.ca
Bolton, ON

25732434R00166